The Last Checkpoint

By the same author

To Remember With Tears

The Bitter Lollipop

The Secret Soldier

The Golden Stream

John Quigley

The Last Checkpoint

Collins
St James's Place, London,
1971

*The characters and incidents in this story are entirely fictitious
and any resemblance to living persons is coincidental*

ISBN 0 00 221480 6

© John Quigley 1971

Printed in Great Britain
Collins Clear-Type Press
London and Glasgow

Author's Note

The aquarium and reptile house which provides the background to one chapter of this novel is not the Aquarium and Reptile House of the famous West Berlin Zoo, although for the purposes of the story it is set in the same part of the city.

Book One

Chapter One

It was not yet five o'clock but the lounge of the Hotel Unter den Linden was crowded and smoky. Another tall blonde came in and joined the four or five well-groomed fräuleins already mixing with the Indonesian saboteurs, the Arab trade unionists, the pineapple salesmen from Cuba. Officially, it was external fraternal relations. There was a small Government department for it.

The fat barman rattled a few cocktails. Some were golden and some were green but they tasted pretty much the same, Margaret knew, whatever the colour; whether the base was 'Scotch' whisky made in Leipzig or 'London' gin as local as the Brandenburg Gate.

She was digging with a spoon in the dark brown sediment that glistened like paint in her otherwise empty cup.

'You know, Walter,' she said thoughtfully, 'there's still an awful lot of coffee in Brazil. Real coffee. Couldn't you spare just a little foreign currency to buy some?'

Eisler smiled uncomfortably. The country and its shortcomings kept coming between them like an awkward parent.

'Soon you won't know the difference,' he said. 'You'll prefer that to coffee.'

A small, bespectacled hero on a propaganda trip from North Vietnam came out of the automatic lift and padded warily across the red carpet as if it might be mined. His navy-blue suit looked as if he had swum the Mekong River in it and his hair might not have been combed since he last ran out of a burning village with the Marines after him. He looked bemused by all the noisy solidarity.

'I suppose,' Margaret said, her expression suggesting that she was giving it serious thought, 'I suppose people do eventually forget what things are really like. If they didn't they would go mad. It also makes them fairly easy to subjugate.'

Eisler followed her meaningful examination of the hotel lounge, its occupants and its activities, trying not to be too provoked by her teasing, trying to see it as it would seem to her.

'I know what you're thinking,' he said. 'That here, in a Socialist country, we are perpetuating some of the less endearing abuses of Capitalism.'

He was pleased, if slightly surprised, to hear her laugh.

'Perpetuate is hardly the word, Walter. Resurrect would be more accurate. The wicked Capitalists gave up this sort of thing years ago. I mean, apart from the fact that the coffee is a fraud and that most of the allegedly imported drinks are a confidence trick, just look at those poor girls. They look quite nice kids. If it isn't a rape of human dignity to put them in bed with Abdul and Ho so that Abdul and Ho will go home with wonderful memories of the German Democratic Republic, then I don't know what is.'

'They are expressly forbidden to do that,' he said. 'They are hostesses in the most innocent sense of that word.' He realised with a pang that in truth he did not know the extent of the girls' duties. Perhaps Margaret was right. He must inquire.

'Oh, sure.' She made a disbelieving face.

He watched his bodyguard leave the table he was at and move to another, just vacated, from which he would have a better view of the long room. The man was wearing an overcoat of the speckled fawn tweed that had been the year's big production pattern at the V E B mills. The length of the coat accentuated his smallness. More than once Eisler had heard it laughingly said that to get a job in the Ministry of State Security you had to be as dwarfish as Julius Bahr, the Minister. It couldn't be true. It was the sort of libel that the editor of *Neues Deutschland* – if drunk – might risk a sly cartoon about. Nevertheless . . .

Margaret was also watching the bodyguard. She said: 'I suppose Comrade Zander will put all this in his reports? I mean, me . . . and you.'

'It's not his job.'

She caught the man's eye as he rustled over a page of his newspaper. She smiled at him. After a moment of blankness a slow, shy, almost disapproving return smile moved across the big-eyed face. It was, Margaret thought, an interestingly irregular face, cut diamond-style as if to reflect many moods.

Eisler sensed the man's embarrassment. 'You're supposed to pretend he isn't there,' he said.

'I know, but I feel so sorry for him, always sitting on his own. He's got the eyes of a lost child.'

'I've always thought them vacant.'

'I'm always meaning to buy him another newspaper.' Her expression was mischievous again. 'That one's getting terribly tattered.'

Eisler smiled. 'Yesterday he was reading Robert Burns.'

'Well, I don't suppose they'll shoot him for that. Burns was pretty hot on the federation of man.'

'Our children read Burns at school,' he said reprovingly.

She put her chin on her hand. 'I wonder if he could really protect you? He looks so fragile.'

'Apart from the gun in his pocket he's trained to kill bare-handed.'

She shuddered. 'Stop, before you put me off him.'

One of the well-dressed girls went out followed by two

beaky Arabs dressed in tight powder-blue suits and orange-tinted shoes. The tousle-haired hero from Hanoi padded back the way he had come, looking as if he would rather have been crawling about the Demilitarised Zone.

'Has anyone spoken to you about me, yet?'

The tables were well spaced but she had switched from German to English.

Eisler turned quickly in his chair so that he was facing her more directly. Her brown hair looked soft and warm in contrast to the faded eyes, the slight sharpness of face and angularity of figure that often hallmarks the American woman on a permanent diet.

'No,' he said. 'Why should they?' He tried to sound only politely interested.

She was staring into the coffee grounds as if reading them.

'There's a paragraph about me in *Neues Deutschland* to-day. It's headed, *The American Woman,* and it reads like something out of early Hedda Hopper. It doesn't actually mention you but there are some very strong hints.'

'I saw it,' he said, looking carefully beyond her to a gleaming green cocktail passing on a tray, in a glass frosted and rimmed with sugar. 'It could have referred to any of half a dozen ministers. Telephone the editor to-morrow and let him know you're researching for a book on Nazi war crimes. You never know, he might be able to open a few doors you haven't thought of.'

She pushed her cup away with a sigh. 'What's the use of pretending, Walter? If we go on like this there's bound to be a scandal.' His silence seemed to exasperate her. 'Well, isn't there?'

It was an insidious invitation which he felt he must on no account accept this evening. He would need all his nervous energy for the meeting of the Praesidium.

'My dear.' He kept his voice light. 'You seem to live in

perpetual awareness of scandal. Is it your newspaper training or a lurid past?'

She responded with a half smile, but her tone was insistent.

'I'm only thinking of the harm this could do you. We shouldn't be sitting together in the public lounge of one of the busiest hotels in East Berlin.'

After to-night, he thought sadly, we may never be able to do it again. Four months ago, on his election as First Secretary of the Party and Chief of State, he had told the Central Committee: 'I will not have my face displayed on the hoardings or pasted round lamp-posts. I do not want my birthday celebrated with lengthy tributes in the Press or pledges of higher output from the workers. I hope there will be no songs or poems in my honour.' It had been a tilt at the gruesome paternalism of his predecessors. So far, his wish had been respected. Since his election, his photograph hadn't appeared more than three or four times in *Neues Deutschland*. His forty-third birthday had been recorded in a three-line sentence. The reticence had not gone unnoticed in the West. He had appeared on the front cover of *Time* as *The Unknown Dictator* and *Bild* had labelled him *The Invisible Man of Pankow*. But the precious privacy could not last much longer now. To-night's speech to the Praesidium would probably kill it forever. He dwelt for a few uncomfortable moments on the chances of it killing more than his private life. In 1965, Erich Apel, Walter Ulbricht's Finance Minister, had preached a liberalisation programme not one tenth as daring as the plan Eisler was going to propose. In the end, the pressures had become so cruel that Apel had put a bullet through his own head.

Apel dead.

Before him, Gerhart Ziller.

Who next for the roll of honour?

Eisler said: 'So far as anyone is concerned, Margaret, we are dear old friends. Even the First Secretary of the S E D is allowed that.'

'Dear old guilty friends. Dear old guilty worried friends,' she said with emphasis.

'I don't feel guilty. I'm a bachelor. You're a widow.'

'I'm also an American,' she said. 'You know that's what's worrying me. You must know even better than me how dangerous it is.' Her face softened. 'And because of that I'm very touched and flattered.'

He said quietly: 'I love you, Margaret. It's as simple and as wonderful as that.'

For a moment he thought she was going to protest, but she went steadily on: 'I can just imagine the outcry there would be back home if someone discovered that the President had a girl friend from behind the Iron Curtain.'

'Even if your President sincerely loved this girl and wanted to marry her?'

In a sudden, protective movement she leaned forward and put both hands on his arm. 'Walter, I've told you that can never happen. Being the husband of *The American Woman* would destroy you. The best way I could show my love would be for me to leave this country to-morrow. But . . .' she shook her head as if in apology '. . . I want to stay with you.'

He could feel the warmth of her hands through the thin cloth of his jacket sleeve. 'After to-night I'm going to need you more than ever.'

There was a burst of laughter from the bar where some off-duty waitresses and the head porter, with a raincoat over his uniform, were drinking with the guests.

Margaret leaned back into the brown upholstery of the characterless modern chair as if realising that their tense attitude would attract attention. 'Why is to-night's meeting so important?'

'Now, if I told you that before telling them, they really would have reason for complaint.'

She pouted a little. 'Only if they knew you'd told me.'

He hesitated and then shrugged. 'I'm going to propose some changes.'

'For the people out there?' She nodded towards the reconstructed street, where now the raw buildings were mellowing a little in the fading light and the new young linden trees, wrapped in their cassocks of straw, were trembling in the November wind. 'They could do with a few changes. I hope they're for the better.'

It suddenly seemed immensely important to him that Margaret should be the first to know. He said: 'Would you agree that life in Berlin is dominated by the Wall?'

'I don't think anyone would deny that.'

'Well, I don't think we need the Wall any more. One of the things I want to do is take it down. That's one of the reasons why to-night's meeting is so important.'

Even saying it quietly, just to her, made him feel slightly breathless and strangely guilty.

'Take down the Berlin Wall?'

She was startled. The whole world would be startled. He said:

'The Wall is an affront. To the Party, to the country, to the whole idea of human dignity.' His voice had become angry. He might have been talking to a larger, less receptive, audience. He leaned closer to her. 'I hate it, Margaret, for the people who have died on it and for what it symbolises to the world. If we still need the Wall then our Socialism has failed. If we do not need it then it should not be there.'

He wondered with mild alarm if lip-reading might be one of the esoteric arts that Comrade Zander had been trained in.

'The Praesidium will never agree with you,' she said.

All at once, he felt indescribably alien. It was as if the saboteurs and the pineapple salesmen had inherited the earth. He had known this hotel since it was built but now he found himself looking about as he might have done on his first visit, when he hadn't known where anything was or where all the doors led.

She touched his hand. 'Did you hear me, Walter?'

'Yes,' he said, 'but I'm confident that the Praesidium will agree with me.' He was conscious of sounding very formal. 'A majority of them, anyway.'

'Then the Russians won't let you.'

He looked at her as if she had struck him. 'You can't say that.' His voice was almost pleading. 'We don't know what the Russians will do.'

She stared at him in disbelief and said: 'I'll bet I know.'

Chapter Two

He had told them.

He wound down the window of the car and looked across the blackness of the Tiergarten to West Berlin, to the lights of the Europa Center, the Hilton Hotel, the Mercedes building; fancying that he could hear the distant roar of Capitalism, liking it, envying them their possession of it. Was this another counter-revolutionary thought, or just an ordinary human one? *Transforming hearts and raising hands in the name of Man's honour, that is what I call Revolution.* He wished that he had remembered these words of Marx during the meeting so that he might have quoted them to Karl Zetkin.

He smiled a little in the darkness. It was ironic that Zetkin should pose as the keeper of the Party's conscience. He was certainly the flamboyant defender of its orthodoxy, rearing up at the first whisper of ideological deviation; but that was something quite different.

It was Walter Ulbricht who had recruited Zetkin from the editor's chair of *Neues Deutschland* and told him to tame the intellectuals. Zetkin had purged, and was still purging, with enthusiasm. The irony to Eisler was that Zetkin was a cynic, possibly even a sceptic. Above all he was an opportunist. Eisler knew that the least he could expect from Zetkin was open opposition; more probably, treachery.

The dark mound of Hitler's bunker slipped past on the right and on the left there appeared the blue light of a watchtower overlooking the death strip and the Wall beyond. A match flared in the front of the car as Comrade Zander lit two cigarettes and handed one to the driver.

Eisler closed the window and leaned back into the soft upholstery that was to be found only in official cars. He thought again: *Now they all know.* Any of them who imagined that they had installed an amenable puppet could think it no longer. He had given them his thoughts quietly and briefly and then ended the proceedings without discussion or vote, adjourning for a week so that they might consider his proposals.

Despite the inconclusive nature of the meeting he judged it to have been a success. Including himself, the Praesidium had twelve members.

Ten of them had shaken his hand as he left; some of them perhaps a little hesitantly, like old Albert Behrens, or downright unconvincingly, like Julius Bahr. Nevertheless, only Karl Zetkin had been diplomatically engaged on the telephone.

A memory came back to him of Zetkin's eyes, very hard and inquiring in the straight-nosed English gentleman's face. Again he heard the sarcastic voice: 'I am so glad we are not a meeting of writers or artists. Otherwise, Julius might have to arrest us all.'

Julius Bahr had laughed uncomfortably and stretched himself up another notch, extracting the last centimetre of advantage from his little spine.

Eisler had said: 'Have you a guilty conscience about something, Karl?' He had never at any time paid Zetkin the compliment of publicly taking his posturings seriously. Banter was the best weapon against Zetkin. 'Perhaps that beautiful suit you are wearing. It doesn't look to me like DDR cloth.'

Zetkin's manner could not have been more relaxed. 'I always have a guilty conscience about something or

18

other, Walter, but that is not quite the point. Are you perfectly happy that what you have been proposing doesn't amount to counter-revolution?'

'Karl, you are a romantic. We never had a revolution.' Zetkin had poured himself a glass of water. 'I was always taught that the Revolution of 1917 was for the workers everywhere.'

Eisler's tart reply had uncovered a vein of support for his proposals deeper and richer than anything he had dared hope for. 'I am a Communist, Karl, but I am also a German. And Karl . . .' he had leaned forward for emphasis '. . . I am a German first.'

There had been such a burst of approval for this rebuke that Zetkin had choked back, in obvious surprise, whatever taunt he had been preparing to throw next.

The car swung out to pass an old, crocodile-snouted bus which grunted noisily and emptily towards the outer darkness of the city. As the car resumed its position Eisler leaned forward and tapped the driver's shoulder. 'Stop here, please. I will walk from here.'

The lights were poor and the shadows many in Otto-Grotewohl-Strasse, but no more so, he thought, than in any other part of the German Democratic Republic. It was his job now to get rid of the shadows. He stood for a moment pulling on his gloves as the Trabant moved down the empty street with the exhaust vapour writhing in the glow of the tail lights. A wind tipped with snow was blowing across the Tiergarten and as the swirling chill caught at his breath he momentarily regretted having abandoned the warmth of the car. Then he reminded himself that this might be the last time he would be able to take a solitary walk like this; solitary, that was, if one could forget Comrade Zander, the man from the *Staatssicherheitsdienst*, trailing twenty paces behind, the gun in one pocket, the folded newspaper in another. Like his meetings with Margaret, the walks might soon have to be transferred to less public places.

Somewhere over by the Wall a police dog barked. Pools of light from the watchtowers moved about the death strip, crossing and re-crossing the empty grass and the rows of white dragon's teeth. At this distance, in the moving lights, the Wall itself looked deceptively low. That, he thought, was probably how it had looked to the men and women who had died trying to get over it. In his heart there was a cross to every one of them.

He walked over the empty concrete in front of the Brandenburg Gate and turned into Unter den Linden, walking towards the scene of last week's bomb incident at the Soviet Embassy.

Already the two bullet holes in the silver linden tree in front of the main entrance had been neatly plugged with plastic wood coloured to match the rest of the slender stem. The tree would live. One of the demonstrators had been less lucky. He had been buried that morning.

Lights were burning from one end of the embassy's 600-foot frontage to the other. No doubt by to-morrow morning they would have a précis of his speech, prepared by Zetkin or possibly Julius Bahr, and by to-morrow night it would be in Moscow on Kozhnev's desk. Eisler had been reared without a belief in God. Sometimes now he wondered if he any longer believed in Man.

He thought again of his old chief, Erich Apel, as he had found him that morning in 1965 lying dead across his office desk with the gun still in his hand. Apel had been almost alone in his fight for reform. He had been a man in advance of the times. Was this now a better time? Eisler hoped so.

Chapter Three

Eisler had a small town apartment on the second floor of a grey, shrapnel-marked building which had been the headquarters of Goebbels' anti-Russian propaganda division and which now housed the Department of External Trade. He had retained it since the days when this had been his Ministry. He preferred it to his official villa in the fortified residential compound for high State officials which lay behind another wall on the northern fringe of the city. The unpredictability of his domestic arrangements was further complicated by the fact that he sometimes slept on a fold-down bed in his office at Central Committee Headquarters. Several times Julius Bahr had complained to him about the added security problems created by these irregular bachelor habits.

To-night, when he reached the flat, Albert Behrens was waiting for him. A visit from the old man was not unusual in itself, except that they had been together not much more than half an hour ago at the meeting of the Praesidium.

Behrens was sitting by an electric fire, reading, his eyes wrinkling in a cloud of sour brown smoke from the low-grade patriotic pipe tobacco that he insisted on using. He had a fringe of white hair which curled out above his ears. Only the paleness of his complexion kept his appearance from being benign. He wore his pallor like a decoration, claiming that it had been acquired in a Nazi prison. Eisler sometimes wondered if it might not have been accentuated by the time Behrens had spent crouching in an exile's apartment in Moscow during the years of the

21

Stalin purges. To-day Albert Behrens was Chairman of the Central Party Control Commission. At an official function to mark his fiftieth year in the international Socialist movement he had described himself as a 'mild old Party horse who does a lot of grazing nowadays but very little galloping.' Nevertheless, when Albert Behrens spoke the Party was inclined to listen out of respect as well as affection.

One of Eisler's earliest memories was of his father and Albert Behrens bent over the kitchen table writing their weekly anti-Hitler articles for a Communist news sheet which had at that time circulated illegally among the factory workers of Berlin.

He said: 'Why didn't you tell me you were coming, Albert? We could have driven over together.'

Behrens blew a cloud of smoke, then bent and switched off one bar of the fire before answering. 'Because I didn't want us to travel together, Walter.'

'That sounds ominous.'

Eisler studied the old man with affection. His double-breasted blue suit looked as if it had been bought many years ago, second-hand, somewhere down at the bottom end of the Damneralleestrasse. He was a terrible advertisement for Communism but it would have been cruel to try to change him now.

Eisler opened two bottles of beer and said casually: 'Now tell me what you really thought of to-night's meeting.'

Behrens blinked tolerantly through a puff of smoke that seemed to sag with its own weight. 'I think my presence here probably tells you that.'

'You mean you don't approve?'

Behrens waved his pipe. 'Oh, in principle I approve and wish you well, but that does not prevent me having serious doubts and worries.'

Eisler put a hand on the coarse cloth of the ancient suit. 'You have known me all my life, Albert. I don't think I could have been elected without your support. You were the kingmaker. You must have known what my policies were likely to be.'

'I didn't think you would act so quickly. I misjudged you there.' The voice was not so much reproachful as self-reproachful. With a sigh, Behrens tapped his pipe out and put it in a pocket, grimacing a little with stiffness. 'You are a courageous man, Walter, but I must warn you that in the opinion of an old revolutionary the programme you outlined to-night might turn out to be too dangerous for you. You have a businessman's instinct for making a commercial success and the idealist's dream of justice.' He smiled grimly into the shadows as if remembering other men like Eisler. 'An uncomfortable combination, I'm afraid.' He looked regretful. 'You see, Walter, you are not cynical enough. You believe that wrongs should always be righted. That is not politics. Sometimes it is more politic to leave wrongs unrighted.'

Eisler saw his life stretching ahead in a long series of such conversations with different men, each revealing to him things that he would be happier not knowing; about them, about himself.

He said: 'I do not like playing politics, Albert. You are right, I suppose, when you speak of me as a businessman. As a businessman, I see the Wall as bad window-dressing for what the shop has to sell.'

'None of us likes the Wall.'

'As a businessman I keep remembering things about it that probably don't interest you. So far it has cost us 150 million Marks – just for building it, beautifying it, trying to make it look as if it isn't there.'

Behrens nodded approvingly.

'In addition to that,' Eisler went on, 'we need 15,000

border troops to man it. I asked for the upkeep figures on that the other day – at least another twenty million Marks a year.'

'It is the best money we ever invested, or ever will,' Behrens said energetically. 'Before the Wall went up we lost almost four million people. We were being bled white.'

Eisler looked at his hands. Had he always held them like this, clenched till the skin was blotched with white? He said: 'Don't the deaths ever worry you, Albert?'

Behrens had the comfortable look of a man who has spent a lifetime sitting in committee and who is now on the far side of any argument – safe and unreachable. 'The real question is – Can we afford to have another exodus? Are you willing to go back to the situation as it was?'

'Things have changed since the Wall was built. I don't believe all that many people would want to leave now.'

The old man's teeth worked irritably on the short-stemmed pipe. 'But you can't be sure, can you? To me the Wall seems a small price for the D D R having become the fifth strongest industrial power in Europe.'

Eisler put his beer glass down with a thump and gave an exaggerated groan of protest.

'Why must we always fall back on the materialist argument, Albert? This is the Communist tragedy. We are always willing to put our humanity blindfold against a wall and shoot it when it suits us.'

Behrens' gaze was stolid. He was by trade a maker of bread and when necessary his manner could become as dry and dusty as the inside of an old-fashioned bakehouse.

Eisler closed his eyes and tried to think of the system as Behrens was seeing it; as he had at one time been able to see it himself. Fallible but paternal; cumbersome but sure; ruthless, perhaps, but only in its infinite wisdom.

Behrens finished his beer noisily. When he spoke his

voice was more solemn. 'I suppose you know what this could do to your career?' Suddenly his manner became agitated. 'You are so vulnerable, Walter. You are too young to have any great fund of Party loyalty to fall back on in a crisis. And in addition . . .' he looked embarrassed '. . . forgive me for mentioning it, but you are apparently being unwise enough to throw your private life open to suspicion.'

Eisler flushed. The room had suddenly become intolerably warm. He reached down and flicked off the radiator. He tried to keep the anger from his voice. 'What are they saying about me?'

'Oh, this . . . American woman . . . this writer.'

'Margaret Sloane is her name. What about her?'

'I don't know, but . . .' the old man spread his hands appealingly '. . . surely you cannot be so optimistic as to imagine that such a liaison will not give offence?'

'I don't see why it should. I've known Margaret for years. I have many friends in the West. I met her when I took a trade mission to London.'

'When you left London you should have forgotten her.'

'Albert, I'm in love with her.'

The old man looked flustered. 'My dear boy, that is not an extenuating circumstance. It is a further foolishness. This country is full of adorable women whom you could love in joy and in safety. I have been urging you for years to find a wife. But don't, I beg of you, put a knife into the hands of your enemies by choosing an American. It would be calamitous for you. Especially on top of these other dangerous measures that you propose.'

A small point of pain was beginning to form at the side of Eisler's head. He said: 'Is our system so fragile that it would be threatened if I took an American wife?'

'You distress me, Walter.' Behrens was trying to relight his pipe but the matches kept going out. 'If she was

25

even a well-known Socialist writer from America one could perhaps see possibilities, despite the unfortunate nationality, but I am told she is, on the contrary, a writer for Right-wing journals.'

'She is a wholesome, attractive, intelligent human being. Does the fact that she is an American change all that?'

'In your involvement with her you may think, or hope, that it does not, but do not expect others to see it in the same way. And above all, Walter, do not be blinded by love. It will not escape the notice of those who oppose you that the statement of your liberal ideas coincides with the appearance of this woman. Do not complain if some of them suggest that it was her hand which planted the seeds in your heart.'

This, Eisler thought, was politics, the seizing of every advantage, living off the country as you went along. He had done it himself. It was difficult to sound indignant. 'Everyone who knows me would see that for rubbish.'

'But not everyone knows you.'

Eisler retreated a little. 'Is it generally known about Margaret?'

Behrens smoothed his hands along the fringes of silvery hair. It was a move that suggested weariness. 'Oh, there have been the usual sly smiles but I don't think anyone guesses how serious it is. I would think that those who know still imagine, as I did until now, that it is merely an indiscreet affair. But it will become more widely known very quickly. I have seen you with her. So will others.'

'I didn't know you had seen us, Albert. You should have spoken.' It seemed important that this old friend should actually know what Margaret looked like.

'You were in your car.' Behrens puffed hard at the reluctant tobacco. The memory seemed to perplex him. He took the pipe from his mouth and pointed it accusingly. 'But it was stopped in traffic. I had a very good view.'

Eisler smiled shyly. 'Well, tell me. What did you think?'

'Of your lady?'

'Of course.'

'I don't know. I didn't think much about her to begin with. For a time I thought she was one of us, although I'll admit I was puzzled by her dress. It was only afterwards . . .' He blew a rancid cloud. 'She has character, I suppose. She wears the clothes of a rich foreigner and yet she has the face of a poor student or a conspirator, the face of someone who is still reading or writing when other people are asleep.'

That's right, Eisler thought. It is the face of a student who has grown weary of the exams.

The old man was still speaking. 'You must forgive me, but the type is not one to which I have ever been attracted. She reminds me a little of our intense Party sisters. I never liked them.' He spread his hands. 'But then, I have no taste. I still have the instincts of a village baker.' He laughed. 'I always preferred them to be a little doughy so that I might shape them myself. There did not appear to be anything doughy about Mrs Sloane.'

'There isn't.' Eisler grinned and went for more beer. When he came back he said: 'I must say, she didn't seem to be on anyone's mind to-night.'

Behrens frowned. 'You must please yourself, Walter. Perhaps I am over-painting the situation.'

Eisler held out a packet of cigarettes. 'Try one of these instead of that awful old rubbish bin.' He struck a match. The flame brought a glow of warmth to Behrens' paleness.

'Anyway, Albert, you are warning me that you think I won't get the support I need? That my relationship with Margaret will colour the whole situation?'

'No, at this stage I am quite certain you will get the support you need. As I have said, you are holding out a wonderful vision. It is later that I am worried about.' He sat blinking for a few moments as if puzzled. 'I'll even vote for you myself, but I will pray for you as well.'

Somehow, the reference to prayer seemed more noteworthy than the forecast of success. It was a word that Eisler could not remember having heard for years. 'Pray?'

'Yes. Do I surprise you?'

'A little.'

'I was brought up to pray, Walter, and I've never been able to rid myself of the habit.'

'Does that mean you believe in God?' He spoke the last word awkwardly.

'I don't know.'

'Then who do you pray to?'

'I don't know. I just pray. I've never found that it did any harm.'

Chapter Four

Eastwards, beyond the city, snow was falling, weighing down the long, pliant branches of larch and pine, deadening even further the silence of a countryside in which few cars moved.

In the city, under the Weidendammer Bridge, there was ice at the edges of the Spree and the swans stepped carefully over it as if it might crack with their weight. Two or three delegates from somewhere in Africa shivered their way across Bertolt Brecht Platz towards another seminar which, if pointless, would at least be warm. The signs were of a hard winter. Within a day or two the gas pressure would fall, electricity cuts would plunge whole towns into darkness and by Christmas the coal stocks would be shown, once again, to be inadequate.

Condensation disfigured the windows of Eisler's office, giving the outside scene a cracked and distorted look, as if things had started falling apart. It was only two days since he had spoken to the Praesidium but this morning, as he waited for Karl Zetkin to arrive, his thoughts were of Margaret, and of the prophecy that Albert Behrens had made. *They will say it was her hand which planted these seeds in your heart.*

The wording was quaint but the thought perceptive. Could he deny that it might have something to do with Margaret? He could not deny that she had something to do with his sudden awakening to the world beyond politics, an awakening to such unlikely things, for him, as the beauty of moonlight on a pane of glass seen from the inside of a dark room, or the awful waste of fat rosebuds turning black, unopened, on a frosted bush. It would possibly be more accurate to say that the seeds had always been there but that Margaret had brought them alive. He tried to think back, seeking the door through which doubt, hope, whatever it was, had first entered. What he kept seeing was her face. He felt as he gazed from the weeping window that she stood in a mysterious and inescapable relationship to his future and that he must suffer anything rather than lose her. She was some new sort of delegate in a country of delegations, incongruously arrayed in the clothes and perfumes of New York and the accents of Boston. He had an immense wish for her to be there beside him so that they might face Zetkin together.

*

Zetkin came, as Eisler had expected, with a proposal for compromise. He smelled, as usual, of some toilet preparation far too subtle to have been manufactured anywhere in Communist Europe and the cigarettes he held out were English.

There was no offence in having either but it was interesting to Eisler that hardly anything about Zetkin could be bought in a shop anywhere in the D D R except by visitors in possession of U S dollars. His ability to acquire the trappings of a society he professed to abhor was revealing, but not nearly so revealing as his wish to acquire them.

At the first pause in the conversation Eisler said blandly: 'That's not the suit you were wearing at the meeting on Tuesday night, Karl?' An enemy whom you can ridicule, however quietly, never seems so troublesome.

Zetkin preened himself a little. 'No. Do you like it? It's English worsted.' He stroked it. 'I know an old tailor who has the odd suit length brought in by relatives from the West. He always gives me first refusal.'

'You must take me to him, some time, Karl. Your appearance is a credit to the Government and to the Party.'

Zetkin took it, gravely, as a compliment.

We are all of us, Eisler thought sadly, possessed of a monstrous effrontery in seeking power. We are as fickle, fallible, vain and helpless as the people whose lives we dare to shape.

'It is one of the small changes I would like to see taking place,' he said. 'Our people are drab. It is not a good advertisement for us. We should give ourselves a better image.'

Zetkin seemed to realise that he had been side-tracked.

'Freedom of the Press,' he said bluntly, as if challenging Eisler to change the subject again, 'is a wonderfully idealistic dream. And one, of course, that we all share. Naturally, we would all like to set the Press free.' His voice hardened. 'But some of us are more realistic than others. Some of us can see that we daren't set the Press free. It is an unfortunate imperfection of our system.' He smiled faintly. 'All systems have their imperfections. In ours the gains far outweigh the losses.'

But for whom, Eisler asked himself? The people or the Party?

He said: 'I am sorry, Karl, that you have so little faith in the Government that you think it would crumble if exposed to a little unhindered comment.'

Zetkin shrugged, and the well-tailored jacket moved as if it was part of him. 'I see no wisdom in putting a weapon in the hands of our enemies.'

'Western countries seem to survive.'

'Unlike them we are fighting an ideological war. In war one does not give away advantages.' He put a hand over his eyes as if weariness had overtaken him. 'And talking about war, it would be as well to remember that we have twenty divisions of Russian troops stationed in the DDR.' His voice was vaguely petulant. 'I could not support any action which might set armoured tanks rolling against the East German people.'

It was the thought which troubled Eisler most. How *would* the Russians take it? Marx, Lenin, Grotewohl and Ulbricht watched from the far wall like the communion of saints. He said quickly: 'I do not believe the Soviet Union would ever violate our sovereignty.'

Zetkin leaned forward, picking at something on his sleeve. 'Why risk it by moving far too quickly?'

Eisler sank back in his chair. Zetkin was being more reasonable than he had expected. 'Tell me which points trouble you most?'

'The Press. The Western-style Opposition in the *Volkskammer*. The Wall.'

Eisler nodded almost with sympathy. 'I know, Karl, I know. We all have a strong instinct for self-preservation. I have it, too, believe me. But these changes must come. One day they will come even in the Soviet Union.'

'Your greatest strength in presenting these proposals for Moscow's approval . . .'

Zetkin stopped as Eisler struck the desk angrily. 'We are not required in this country to submit our plans to a foreign government.'

Zetkin bowed a little. 'All right. Your greatest strength in forcing through any programme of reform should come from the knowledge that you have carried everyone with you, that you have behind you a united Praesidium.'

Eisler pressed a button and asked his secretary to come in before he turned again to Zetkin. 'In politics, Karl, unanimity is a very rare bird. I don't think I can wait to see it.'

Chapter Five

The head of Julius Bahr, Minister of State Security, jerked about on his narrow shoulders as he flapped the letter in front of Eisler. He said: 'I know you'll appreciate how embarrassing this is for me.'

Eisler often wondered why Bahr did not have a limp. It seemed to be about the only thing that had been over-looked. Or perhaps the limp was inside, in his mind.

If Karl Zetkin was the handsomest member of the Praesidium – and the factory girls of Dresden had recently voted him so – then Bahr was the ugliest. His skin had a dry and dusty quality which at first glance made it look as if he might have spent too long under a sunray lamp and was having to wear a dilute solution of calamine lotion. His ears were too big for his thin, hollowed face and in a democracy the newspaper cartoonists would have shown these as controlling the man. The lips were firm but so pale and cold looking that it was difficult to imagine any woman ever kissing them, although it was said that many had.

To-day, Julius Bahr had a cold and in the heat of the room he began to cough, looking almost grateful for the diversion this created. Eisler decided not to be helpful. He waited, saying nothing, but thinking – *So it has started already. The psychological warfare. The subtle onslaught on the nerves.*

Eventually Bahr had to go on. 'You understand, Walter, it has been forced upon me.' He handed the letter across the desk. 'I must act.'

Eisler nodded. 'Oh, yes, I understand.' He lifted the letter. 'It's anonymous, I see.'

Bahr apologised with his wet eyes. 'Most of our information comes that way.' His bony shoulders raised themselves a little. 'It is understandable.' He paused. 'Of course, if you were to say the information is false, that you do not know the lady . . .'

'Oh, no. As far as it goes, the letter is quite accurate. Of course I know Mrs Sloane. And I can vouch for her. But I know that won't do. Everything must be done in the proper way.'

Bahr wriggled as if to levitate. He was never happy away from his own room and the long-legged chair that put him on the same level as other men.

'You must believe, Walter, that my inclination was to burn this letter, but . . . there is a procedure for these things.'

Eisler thought: How symbolic are those big ears, Julius. No one in East Germany can have had to listen to more instances of man denouncing man than you.

'Files are kept, Walter. Entries are made. Before it reached me at all there was a record of this letter and its contents which even I would find it difficult to destroy. Later . . . if it could be shown that no action had been taken . . . it could be very awkward.'

Eisler leaned forward with a grim smile. 'Don't by shy, Julius. You mean, later . . . if it should turn out that Mrs Sloane is an enemy of the State.'

One of Bahr's small white hands clawed the air. 'Please. I am trying to be as delicate as my duty will allow. I had hoped you would understand. However, if you will instruct me in writing to proceed no further I will see that Mrs Sloane is not troubled.'

The pale lips were pouting round a microscopic fragment of cigarette. Eisler had never seen Bahr with a whole cigarette.

Maybe he cut them in half before lighting up or collected them from ashtrays when other people had finished with them – visiting millionaires, perhaps, because at seven Marks for twenty no East German ever left more than a few centimetres unsmoked.

He said: 'I wouldn't for a moment consider giving you such an improper instruction. But as a matter of interest, doesn't the fact that Mrs Sloane was given an entry visa mean that she is perfectly acceptable to us?'

'She came supposedly to work on a book on Nazi war crimes. Naturally, we were pleased to assist. There was no suggestion then that she might spend some of her time in . . . in very high places.'

'I hope I don't have to assure you that I never discuss affairs of State with Mrs Sloane. She spends most of her time at Potsdam going through the official archives. She has no possible access to secrets. However, she must be treated no differently from anyone else. I insist on that.'

Bahr jerked about apologetically. 'It is normal procedure with anyone likely to be on . . .'

'Yes, yes.'

He watched Bahr bracing himself.

'Before troubling you with this, Walter, I made some harmless inquiries.' Bahr squeezed out an apologetic grimace. It came reluctantly, bubbling a little, like toothpaste from an almost empty tube. 'I found that Mrs Sloane had interviewed such people as Fidel Castro and Che Guevara.'

Eisler nodded as if he had read the interviews. In fact, he had seen very little that Margaret had written.

'Her approach was rather irreverent.' Bahr patted his knee as if it was a dog needing comfort.

'Yes?'

'For instance, she called Castro a bearded bully.'

'No!'

Bahr looked confused at Eisler's amused expression. 'Mrs Sloane has also written from time to time on such subjects as the workers' struggle in Vietnam and Indonesia. She does not seem to sympathise with their aspirations.'

Eisler came out from behind his desk and stood over his Minister of State Security with an expression balanced between anger and contempt.

'That is the sort of stupid intolerance I would like to see us getting away from, Julius. Simply because a person does not wholeheartedly agree with every manifestation of Socialism in every single country of the world it does not necessarily mean that they wish to overthrow the Government of the DDR.'

'There is only one class struggle.' Bahr's voice was stubborn. More than ever his face suggested not so much a ceaseless battle against illness as a complete capitulation to it. Even Eisler, who knew that Bahr's health was excellent, sometimes found himself wondering, as now, if, under the surface, something might not be eating the man away.

'Solidarity is the greatest weapon that the working class has,' Bahr said.

Eisler closed his eyes. He had used the phrases himself, many times. He could not bring himself to scorn them now. He could only hope that he had been able to make them sound less shabby. It had never been, for him, a class struggle, but he had, shamefully, perhaps, used the prescribed war cries. There had seemed little future in being a Protestant in Spain. Had it really been as cynical as that? Certainly, he had never possessed the sublime conviction of an Albert Behrens, who had kept his faith intact through persecution not only by the Gestapo but by the Ogpu, and would have gone to a martyr's stake for it.

His threatening stance beside Bahr relaxed. He turned away and said: 'How are these security checks made? It's something I've never interested myself in.' There was a lot of dirty work that he had never interested himself in. It wasn't much of a defence.

'By straightforward questioning. There is nothing frightening about it.'

'I don't think Mrs Sloane frightens easily.'

'You could be present if you wished.'

'No. I'm sure she wouldn't want that.'

'It would be more discreet, perhaps, if she came to my office. She could be calling there in the course of her researches.'

Eisler resented the vague suggestion that they were, somehow, partners in a conspiracy, but he did not speak.

Bahr said, 'I will make a point of being present myself, as a courtesy.' He took out a pocket diary. 'I could take her next Wednesday afternoon at three.' He might have been a hairdresser accommodating a favoured client. He smiled reassuringly as he put the diary back in his pocket. 'The information once taken will be securely filed. I am sure there will never be any need for us ever to refer to it.'

That's right, Eisler thought. You just want to get me worried. For the first time he felt slightly fearful of the future as he watched Julius Bahr leave the room with his big ears and his mental limp.

Chapter Six

The office in West Berlin from which Ramsden Derby took his orders was in Finckensteinallee between a shop selling wooden figurines from Oberammergau and another offering international automobile insurance to U S servicemen garrisoned in the barracks across the road. *Real Special*, a sign in the Oberammergau shop said in English. *All Ranks*, *All Ages*, the insurance office said.

Ramsden Derby opened the brown-painted door between the two and went up the gritty stone stair to the first floor.

Woolcott's room was the only one with a window overlooking the street. Woolcott spent a lot of time just standing at the window.

He seemed drawn to the view, which opened out beyond the grey barracks wall on to a line of small shops dealing in perfumes and ladies wear, and then to a row of ornate old terrace houses with gables, bubble-glass windows and red roofing-tiles.

This morning, Woolcott was not at the window. He was at his desk, filling a pipe that appeared to be made of opalescent glass.

Derby took off his furry, Russian-style hat. His thin black hair was plastered flat and distributed over his scalp with care. There was a smell of new paint in the room. Derby looked about and made an approving face. It was said that when Woolcott opened the bureau he had declined to have new furniture installed or the rooms redecorated. On the pretext of saving money he had filled the place with old tables and chairs and shelving made of used wood in an effort to suggest an organisation of some antiquity. Now, after eighteen months, he seemed willing to risk a few tins of paint.

'I like your new colour scheme,' Derby said. 'It makes the place look bigger.'

Woolcott smiled. 'It's not much, but it'll do meantime. They're still making me work on a very meagre budget, but with a young organisation that's only to be expected.'

One of the recurring questions in Derby's life was, where had Woolcott been before? It wasn't the kind of thing you could ask in this work. For a time he had felt a strange compulsion to address Woolcott as *Doctor*. But doctor of what? Certainly not medicine. Divinity? He had constructed various other backgrounds for him – diplomatic, scholastic, military – and had abandoned them. There was something about Woolcott that suggested he was almost of his own creation. It was eerie.

'Well,' Woolcott said, 'what have you been able to dig out for me about Herr Eisler?'

Ramsden Derby threw his hat on to one chair and sat down on another; carefully, as if he expected Woolcott to kick it from under him with one of his long telescopic legs. Woolcott spent his life kicking chairs from under people. Derby supposed he wasn't any better, except that possibly he didn't enjoy it quite so much as Woolcott did.

'Just routine stuff,' Derby said. His puffy face puckered a little with effort as he reached for a pocket inside his coat. He produced a sheet of paper and studied it moodily. 'If you take one of these East European politicians you take them all,' he said. 'It depresses me . . .'

Woolcott nodded absently, his eyes straying towards the window.

'Eisler was apprenticed to a toolmaker when he left school and studied at nights for an engineering degree,' Derby said. 'He fought on the Eastern Front when he was sixteen. The Russians captured him and indoctrinated him in a prison camp. He was ripe for it, I suppose. His father had been one of the Communists active against Hitler. After the war Eisler stayed on voluntarily to help reassemble German factories that had been shipped to Russia as reparations. After three years at the Higher Party School in Moscow he went back to East Germany. He joined the *Sozialistische Einheitspartei Deutschlands* and soon became a candidate member of the Praesidium. After a while he was elected to the Holy of Holies itself and given the job of heading its economic commission. At the age of thirty-one he became chairman of the State Planning Commission and Deputy Chairman of the Council of Ministers.'

Derby felt his face going hot as he realised that Woolcott was watching him like an examination inspector. Was this another of Woolcott's fatuous bloody tests? He stopped. Woolcott looked surprised. 'Go on,' he said.

'Well, it was about now that Eisler started playing little tricks. He acted the true blue German whenever there was a conflict between doctrine and patriotism. He began to make no secret of the fact that for him the well-being of the DDR came before Marxist-Leninist theory. Before anyone knew what he was at he had squeezed the bureaucrats out of industry and brought in bright youngsters who had been properly trained for the work.' Derby put his sheet of paper on Woolcott's desk. 'There isn't much more. He knows the West well and has lived for months at a time in all the important Western capitals. He's still a confirmed Communist but he seems to believe that he can use Capitalist methods to create a Red heaven.'

'Then he's a fool,' Woolcott said abruptly. He flicked Derby's notes away as if they annoyed him. The gas lighter in his hand flared and for a wild moment Derby thought he was going to set fire to the sheet of paper. What

Woolcott lit was his strange-looking pipe. The pipe sat very straight and central in his mouth and the delicate way he held the thin stem between two fingers suggested opium rather than tobacco. His eyes were half closed.

'Herr Eisler might be an economic whizz-kid,' Woolcott said, 'but politically I'm afraid he's a romantic idiot. It's the only explanation of this . . . daydream . . . of his.' He nodded to a file on his desk. 'The Russians would take the country over before allowing any of that to happen.'

Derby shrugged. 'It may not be true.'

Woolcott got up and leaned heavily on the mantelpiece, looking down at three or four woodcarvings of girls in traditional Bavarian costume.

'It's true, all right. His Praesidium has accepted the whole parcel of idealistic nonsense. They've even put a name to his absurd manifesto. *Our Socialist Future.* Doesn't it sound lovely?'

'It's a tricky situation,' Derby said doubtfully. 'I suppose all our masters can do is encourage him from a distance.'

Woolcott looked angry. 'I think I've told you before, Ramsden. I don't like that word. I'm nobody's servant. Anyway . . .!' He smoked for a few seconds in silence. 'I don't think that should be the line at all. No.' His voice gained emphasis. 'I don't think the governments of the West should encourage Herr Eisler one little bit, even from a distance. It would be far too dangerous.'

He stared musingly into the pipe smoke as if in the perfumed fug he could see a little of the future. 'If they play it right it's a situation in which the West can't help winning. The Russians will *have* to cut Eisler back to size. They'll come out of it as the brutes. I must say I'm going to enjoy watching them squirm.'

'What about the East German people?' Derby's voice was stiff. He still had a few ideals left. 'They might appreciate a bit of Eisler's freedom. Or don't they matter?'

'Of course they matter.' Woolcott waved a regretful hand. 'But when the price is an upset in the balance of power that has kept Europe at peace since 1945, then we've got to make ourselves forget the East German people. We must forget them, Ramsden. There are only seventeen million of them.'

'You don't imagine that freedom in Eastern Europe can be stifled forever, do you?'

Woolcott left the mantelpiece and walked thoughtfully to the window. 'No, I really don't, Ramsden, but we must go on hoping.'

Derby looked startled, then he smiled nervously. 'That's a pretty staggering statement.'

Woolcott gave him a fond, almost approving, smile. Then he sighed and squinted round the edge of the curtain into the wet grey street.

'You see, Ramsden, we can't all be free. It seems to be one of God's nastier requirements that there has to be a balance between freedom and slavery.'

He turned from the window and began walking back to his desk with both hands stretched in front of him as if he were blind.

'Some of us have to be slaves, Ramsden, and so long as it's not us I don't think we should worry too much who it is.'

Derby rose from his seat. 'Did I tell you I've met Eisler's girl friend? Years ago, in Vietnam, when I was with the C I A.' He looked expectantly across the desk.

'Can't you ever forget you were with the C I A? They're not everything, you know.' Woolcott's voice was petulant.

Derby stared uneasily at him for a moment before lifting his furry hat. 'Sorry,' he said.

Chapter Seven

Eisler spent the first three days of December in Warsaw and was glad when the visit ended. The prevailing atmosphere, even in official quarters, was of depression. Patriotic Poles who wished only to recharge the stagnant economy with new ideas were being denounced as the 'vapid creatures of foreign subversionists'. Everywhere there was a hunt for scapegoats. Men whom Eisler had known for years had disappeared or been demoted and demeaned. The new men looked at him with suspicion. He could not think why until, on his last day, his car was surrounded by a cheering crowd outside the Kyzkawa House. The people came singly and suddenly from doorways and parked cars and converged on his black Volga in a purposeful way that suggested they knew that whatever they were going to do would have to be done quickly. Some of them looked worried and uncertain. As Eisler stepped from his car a girl ran forward and kissed him. Some of the people produced banners and waved them. With amazement he read the slogans. POLAND NEEDS A WALTER EISLER. GOD GIVE STRENGTH TO HERR EISLER. WE WANT IT TO BE OUR SOCIALIST FUTURE TOO.

He stood on the steps of the Kyzkawa for perhaps half a minute, smiling and waving to them in an embarrassed way, and then retreated thankfully into the shadows of the gnarled stone arches. When he came out two hours later there were no demonstrators. Their places had been taken by a large number of policemen. The incident was not mentioned by his hosts and he tactfully made no reference to it himself. But all day it puzzled him. How did the people

43

of Poland know about his plans? In the DDR the public were still uninformed. Only the Praesidium knew officially. No positive moves or even announcements could be made until *Our Socialist Future* had been accepted as policy by the Central Committee of the SED.

He discovered part of the answer in the pages of *Pravda*, which he turned to on the homeward journey. The newspaper carried a long article attacking 'Malignant revisionist tendencies' which were in danger of contaminating the purity of the class struggle in the DDR. No names were mentioned but the 'guardians of the German peoples' democracy' were called upon to repulse an imminent attack from 'highly placed lackeys of the western Imperialist warmongers' – an attack that would be launched in the guise of a glowing future. There was a warning to all who cherished the solidarity of the proletariat to be on their guard against the 'lure of facile theories'. The DDR must not be subverted from the path of progressive international Socialism with the 'cheap bribe of a few worthless dispensations'.

Gobs of cliché-ridden type came spurting up at Eisler through a dull nausea that had little to do with the roughness of the flight. He turned from the newspaper and looked out into total blackness, touching the icy window with his brow. The impenetrable night unnerved him further. Where were the stars? He turned, startled, as a hand touched him on the shoulder. Then he reached out with gratitude for the vodka that one of the party was holding towards him in a paper cup.

Among the people that he had to see next day was Albert Behrens. When they had finished their business the old man lit his pipe and watched interestedly as the fumes billowed out and darkened the room. Then he took a copy of *Pravda* from a bulging pocket and put it in front of Eisler.

'I suppose you've seen this, Walter?'

Eisler nodded. 'I read it last night somewhere over Poland.'

'Well, you can't say I didn't forecast something of the sort.'

'No, but it's come sooner than I would have expected.'

'You could regard it as a warning shot across your bows.'

Eisler smiled confidently. His courage came and went like a fever, lighting him up one day, leaving him drained and troubled the next.

He said: 'A warning shot can usually be counted on to rally the crew behind the captain.'

'Yes, but the follow-up sometimes sinks the ship.' The expression in the mild blue eyes was ironic.

Eisler rose from behind his desk with a chuckle. 'You're a pessimistic old rascal, Albert. Where's the faith that kept you going in prison, and in Moscow, when a footstep in the corridor could mean the Ogpu come to issue you with a travel voucher to Siberia?'

Behrens looked almost grateful for the memory. 'We had a vision of revolution to sustain us then,' he said. 'What we are talking about now is counter-revolution. In that, at least, Karl Zetkin is right.'

Eisler turned his back on the well-posed photographs of his predecessors. 'He isn't, Albert, and neither are you. I also am preaching revolution, but a better revolution.' His voice was gentle. An old man must not be made to feel that a half-century of work was being disparaged. 'I want to make this a country of which we can be truly proud. I want to see Communism with a smile on its face, Albert, and a spring in its step. We've all been glum for far too long.'

At least, he thought, as he watched Behrens leave, wrapped like an ill-tied parcel in his crumpled bag of a suit, to-morrow is Saturday and I will be with Margaret.

45

Saturday was supposed to be a free day but usually it took him most of the morning to extricate himself from even quite routine affairs. To-day, he was tired, short-tempered and anxious to be off. But first, for almost three hours, he had to haggle with two Soviet trade negotiators over the terms they proposed for the sale of crude Soviet oil. The price, Eisler and his advisers knew, was almost forty per cent higher than the world market rate.

In the end, he adjourned the hot-tempered confrontation with nothing resolved and left to rush through a meeting with the Czech ambassador over a border dispute.

After that, he changed into slacks and a tweed jacket in his office, swallowed a bottle of beer and left shortly before one o'clock for Potsdam.

It was here, behind Fritz-Ebert-Strasse, in the cold underground store-rooms of an annexe to the archives centre, that Margaret sat reading, day after day, the records of genocide, mass-murder and human depravity. She arrived with her notebooks and pencils – ink being forbidden – at ten o'clock every morning. At one o'clock she lunched at the Klosterkeller Hotel and worked again in the afternoons until the centre closed at five o'clock.

At first she had lived in Berlin, travelling to Potsdam every day in an uncomfortable double-decker diesel train. Later she rented a small country house that had been State property since the owners were dispossessed. It was three miles from Potsdam in a district of scattered houses served by an unreliable, four-times-a-day bus service. On fine days she sometimes cycled to Potsdam and in the evenings she cooked her own food. There was no one else in the house but an old woman who cleaned and acted as caretaker.

Margaret had a meal ready when Eisler arrived and with it they drank Moselle from West Germany. He had spoken to her only on the telephone since her afternoon

46

with Julius Bahr and when he asked her about the meeting she said:

'I can't think why they bothered. It was more like an interview for a job than a security check. The other man asked all the questions. Julius Bahr just sat there offering me cigarettes and asking if I would like more coffee. They were charming. There was nothing alarming about it.'

Eisler lifted his empty wine glass and squinted at it against the light as if it might be something special. 'No,' he said, 'there wouldn't be. I'm pretty certain it was just a silly bit of theatre designed to alarm me.'

Her hand went out to his.

'Sometimes I get frightened when I think of us.'

'Why?'

'Terrible things can still happen here. To people!' It was almost a question.

He evaded her eyes by leaning forward and throwing another log on the fire. 'Terrible things can happen to people everywhere,' he said moodily.

He felt her fingers tighten. 'Walter, I must know. Do those things still go on?'

A log collapsed in the fire in a flurry of sparks and somewhere outside there was the throaty call of a wood pigeon. He felt flat and shifty as he said: 'What do you mean, Margaret?'

She hesitated and he was terrified that she was going to use the word 'torture'.

'Brainwashing,' she said. 'The things we've all read about.'

It was terrible to be asked. Even more terrible not to know the answer.

There was undeniably a secret police – the SSD. In theory they were answerable for their actions and therefore could not do anything that the law did not permit. In fact, like the secret police everywhere, they were above the law. It was something that they all gladly left to Julius Bahr. They let Julius do their dirty work and hide their worst sins. That he sometimes sanctioned terrible things could hardly be doubted. It was written into his face.

The only words he could speak were the true ones. 'I don't know, Margaret.'

She withdrew her hand from his. 'I hate Communism, Walter. It's difficult to associate you with it.' It was like an accusation and she was immediately regretful. 'I'm sorry. I shouldn't have said that. I seem to keep saying things that hurt you.'

Later, they put on heavy coats and went out. The grass and the trees were thick with rime. Frozen vegetation crackled under their feet and occasionally a startled bird or rabbit clattered about in the brittle undergrowth. The leaves of rhododendron bushes drooped under a thin coating of sugary ice and azaleas stood stark against the grey ground. Through a gap in the trees, far away across very flat country, the late afternoon sun hung red and low in the winter sky. There was a sharp, earthy smell in the still air and already there was a suggestion of gathering mist. In the distance, the windows of a cluster of isolated houses reflected the fiery sun.

He lifted her on to the top spar of a fence and stood behind her, his chin resting on her shoulder, their cold ears touching.

He said: 'It's even more beautiful here in springtime when all these shrubs are in flower. We will come again on the first warm day of spring. That is a promise. Whatever else I should be doing will be cancelled and we will come here to this spot and sit again on this fence.'

She sat staring straight ahead across the vast flatness to the disappearing sun. 'That's a lovely promise for a busy man to make. But it's a dream.'

He enfolded her in a gentle hug and said with deliberate misunderstanding: 'You think I'll forget?'

'I have only another month's work to do at Potsdam,' she said. 'After that . . .' She let the sentence drift.

He felt the day sag and his voice go flat. 'After that . . . what?'

'We knew where things were heading that last time in London. If we'd been sensible we would have finished then.'

He groaned and let his arms slide limply away from her. 'Why must there always be this vision of impermanence?'

She pulled his arms about her again. 'My dear, there's nothing I want more than to stay with you. I'd leave my world gladly and come to your world if that was all that was involved. Being with you would make up for all the shortcomings. If you were a private citizen I wouldn't hesitate. But you're not a private citizen. And we mustn't keep going on about it. We've both known for months that this is how it would be.'

She seemed strong and wise. He was tormented by a sense of his own basic weakness.

'Why must it be? There would be opposition in the Party, I suppose, but the people would love you just as I do.'

'Oh, don't be silly, Walter. The people wouldn't give a damn for me.' Despite the rebuke she was looking at him fondly, almost wonderingly. 'You don't really know very much about people, do you? You've spent far too much time with figures and theories. If the incredible happened and I married you, some of the people would resent me and the rest would be absolutely indifferent.' Her face twisted into a sardonic smile. 'The odd thing is, if you were to marry a real symbol of Western decadence – someone like a Princess Margaret, a Princess Grace or a Jackie Onassis – the people would probably adore her.

People everywhere, but especially in this drab Communist heaven of yours, need a fairy figure to love and imitate; someone who would produce two or three beautiful children with fair hair and lovely smiles. That sort of thing the people would love but not . . .' she made another face '. . . a slightly travel-worn lady with a strange accent and no particular background. I just haven't got the glamour.' She smiled again as she put a hand to her head. 'And already the silver threads are here among the gold.'

The words seemed to mock him as well as herself. 'You're only twenty-seven,' he said desperately. 'We could have children.'

He looked away from her to where the sun splashed winter-red on a large white-painted house on a wooded crag. Smoke, which he could almost smell, and which he was sure would be from birch wood, drifted from one of the chimneys. It looked like a house for contented people.

She jumped lightly from the fence and kissed him. 'Don't spoil things, Walter. I've been longing for this outing. Sometimes down in those dusty old vaults I begin to get the creeps. I feel embalmed. After a week of horror I need the clean goodness of these woods. These last few days, when I came on anything particularly terrible, I kept myself from being ill by remembering that to-day I'd be here with you, knee-deep in frozen bracken.'

'It can't be good for you,' he said sulkily as they started to walk again. 'I can't think why you picked such a gruesome subject as Nazi war crimes.'

'I didn't pick it. It picked me. I was commissioned to do this book. I must earn my living and it's the sort of thing I can do.' Her expression was regretful. 'I have only a very small creative talent but I'm quite a good researcher. Besides . . .' she smiled '. . . I knew it would be the most genuine excuse I would ever have for seeing you again.'

He stopped in surprise. His voice was impatient. 'But my dear, you didn't need an excuse. We don't need excuses.'

She pressed his hand. 'No, not now. Not any more.'

Before he could answer she ran ahead like an exuberant girl, sliding a little on the frozen ground, shouting for him to follow. He watched her slim outline against the old trees. In town her appearance suggested libraries and theatres; the Bode Museum and the Komische Oper. The country changed her. She looked her best out here, as few women would. That troubled face could stand exposure to cold daylight because it had nothing to hide. He shouted a reply and chased after her. There had never been time for anything like this before. Margaret had been right when she had teased him: 'You have devoted yourself to your own advancement with all the deplorable industry of a Capitalist.'

As he crashed through the shrubbery he wondered what Comrade Zander would be thinking of all this. He was nowhere to be seen. He might be small, Eisler thought with a surge of happiness, but he was discreet.

Chapter Eight

Comrade Zander was back in Berlin. He had parked the car beside the television building that looked like a deserted warehouse, crossed the road and walked two or three hundred yards in a westerly direction, passing dingy shops, grey stone walls and apartment buildings that still showed war damage. Despite the neglect, there was a charm about this old quarter that the new concrete and tile areas would never have. Comrade Zander wondered how long it would last. At this hour, when the lights were coming on, fluorescent tubes revealed draughtsmen standing at drawing boards or girls leading customers round showrooms. You could see that most of the houses were no longer homes and realised, with a twinge, that the old high carriage steps at the edges of the pavements were indeed relics which would disappear in the next road development.

Only old people were allowed to live as near to the Wall as this. The windows of the flats showed it in old-fashioned net curtaining and the street itself showed it in an even greater than normal absence of traffic.

The Gerda Kopf Marriage Bureau was on ground floor level behind a door of chipped yellow paint. On one side of it there was a baker's window showing pastry dressed in waxen cherries and pallid cream, and on the other side a shop selling coarse shirts and thick underwear for workmen. The short corridor which led to the bureau was of bumpy wood and the light bulbs were shaded only with dust. The tile walls looked as if someone had been spraying them with machine-gun fire; some unhappy lover, perhaps. Comrade Zander did not like the bare boards. You expected a better surface than this on the bridal path.

Fräulein Kopf was waiting for him in the small distempered room with the hissing gas fire. She was hidden, even on this wintry afternoon, behind sunglasses.

'Poetry,' she said as he went to sit down. 'How sweet.'

Comrade Zander looked puzzled until she held up the enrolment form that he had filled in and posted back to her.

'You've got poetry down here as one of your interests,' she said.

'Oh, yes.'

'You're a romantic, then.' She looked at him approvingly, as if she had a very nice pigeon hole for his kind.

Comrade Zander felt anything but romantic sitting there in his black leather coat, worrying about Eisler, staring into the green mystery of Fräulein Kopf's glasses. Was she trying to symbolise the blindness of love? She was in her middle thirties and her teeth were very white, but what colour were her eyes? He had a sudden, unaccountably strong desire to know what colour her eyes were. He tried to find something else to look at, but there was nothing; a cupboard door with a calendar on it, a telephone, a filing cabinet, a small mirror nailed to the wall.

'This afternoon,' she said, 'I just want to go over one or two points in this Statement of Particulars. For instance, you don't say exactly what it is you do in the State Service. After all . . .' she gave him a smile that could have had meaning if he had wanted to read meaning into it '. . . almost everybody is a State Servant in this country.' Her manner suggested pride that she was one of the few licensed to carry on the Capitalist tradition of private enterprise.

He thought of his first job as a boy in the service of the old Adlon Hotel and said quickly: 'I'm the manager of a wine cellar.' How could he possibly say he was a bodyguard? What girl would want to go out with a bodyguard?

'Managers usually know what they want,' Fräulein Kopf said cryptically.

Comrade Zander wondered, as he often did, what it was he did want, what it was that had made him come here when he read her announcement under the motor car ads in *Neue Zeit*, but the nearest he ever came to an answer was a flickering, magic-lantern shadow of a girl who reminded him strongly of his mother. Was there something wrong with him?

'It's funny I should end up coming to a marriage bureau,' he said, surprising himself with the glib aptness of the thought. 'I mean, when my job is marrying wines.'

For a moment he thought she was going to take her glasses off, but she merely eased them on her sharp, rather attractive nose. 'I didn't know you called it that.'

'It's an old blending expression.'

She looked playful. 'You could say it's my job to produce a good blend, too. We're both working along the same lines.'

As he started to laugh she said: 'Now, you describe yourself in this Statement as Evangelical Church and then go on to say the lady's religion is immaterial to you.' She sounded doubtful.

He nodded. 'I don't care about that sort of thing.' He didn't really care about anything. He was a nominal member of the Evangelical Church for the same reason that he had become a member of the S E D. It made life easier. In the old days he would have been a Nazi.

'But surely you would not want me to introduce you to a . . .' She hesitated and he thought she was going to say *Jew*, but what she did say was '. . . to a Catholic, for example?'

Comrade Zander could not think why not. The room was very warm and his head was beginning to ache. He had driven far too fast from Potsdam without having had any lunch and he still had to get back before Eisler missed him. 'It's immaterial,' he said.

'Well, it's never immaterial to a Catholic, even in our enlightened country.' Fräulein Kopf looked quite severe. 'At the end they always send for a priest.'

She had him a widower already and he hadn't even kissed anybody yet. 'There aren't very many of them about now,' he said, as if they were discussing the dying elephants of Africa.

'That isn't the point, Freddi. They are permitted. I might get some.'

It was a shock to hear her speak his Christian name. People seemed to have been calling him *mister* since he was about fifteen. It seemed that he had been old even at school.

'I'm only trying to guide you, Freddi.'

He glanced anxiously at his watch. 'Change it,' he said, seeing the barriers come down on God knows how many women, among them, perhaps, the one who had been created for him. She was right; he was a romantic; but it must be very recent.

'You're very wise, Freddi,' she said in a satisfied voice that made him realise that it was true what they said about women always getting their own way. She scribbled on the enrolment form. 'You'll find it much more convenient this way.' She smiled and put the form in a folder. 'And, after all, coming to me is a matter of convenience.' Her voice fell. 'Perhaps even of direction.'

Comrade Zander felt the vague confusion that she inspired deepening. 'Of direction?'

'Yes. Don't tell me you don't believe in the Loving Hand that guides us all?'

He had the odd feeling that if he lifted off her dark glasses he would find a very peculiar look in her eyes. 'I've never thought much about it,' he said.

'You ought to. I know that I was guided here.' She looked round the empty little room as if it belonged to someone else. 'If you study your life you'll see that there are times when you are guided. There's someone up there taking an interest in us, all right.' She added quickly: 'It's quite all right for us to believe that, you know. We all have complete freedom of conscience.'

His expression was of total disbelief, blended with slight impatience. As she saw it her manner became businesslike again. 'The point I'm really making is that it's absolutely natural to come to a marriage bureau. After all, some of the greatest love matches of history were arranged.' She looked briskly about her desk and then stood up. 'I'll be in touch with you in a day or two, Freddi, about a first introduction.' She hesitated. 'The girls I have just now are all far too . . . far too tall.' She turned her glasses on him in a concentrated way as if wondering if she might, after all, just risk him with a tall girl.

He felt peculiarly grateful to her. She looked so clean in her white blouse and she made it all sound so normal, as if the enrolment fee and the form-filling were the natural preludes to courtship, and dancing lessons or a wink at the typist the manoeuvres of a pervert.

She was saying: 'Meantime, is there anything you would like to ask me?'

'Yes,' he said. 'You don't think I'm too old?'

'At thirty-three? Of course not. Perhaps a little late in coming to it, but that's not important.' Her face softened. 'What's made you think now of marriage, Freddi?'

He had to admit it was a good question. He had been

putting it to himself for more than a week. The answer had something to do with the way that Margaret looked at Eisler. In Margaret's eyes Comrade Zander had seen a warmth so beautiful that it had almost made him cry for the emptiness of his own life.

'I just thought it was about time I settled down,' he said with a bravura smile that suggested a *galant* wearying at last of unsolemnised adventures.

As he went to the door she said in a reproachful voice, her lips pouting a little in a way that made her look ten years younger, 'You haven't called me Gerda, yet. Not once.'

Dark shutters thudded down in front of Comrade Zander's eyes. 'Gerda,' he said, then floated out into the bullet-riddled corridor feeling like a rapist.

Fräulein Kopf waited until she could no longer hear his footsteps. She unlocked the door that he had taken to be the entrance to a cupboard. Beyond was a small room. She pulled back a carpet, lifted a small trap and went down some steps into a cavity below the floor.

Chapter Nine

It was dark when they reached the house again but a lamp which Margaret had lit before leaving glowed warmly at the small-paned window, silhouetting the red-berried holly wreath that she had hung there. In the garden there was a smell of wood smoke and night air and the trees stood close in the darkness.

'In civilised countries,' Margaret said teasingly, 'people will be starting to think of Christmas.'

Because she had the key she went first. The porch opened directly on to the main room and as she pushed open the second door Eisler heard her cry. Another step and he saw what she saw.

A man in the uniform of a Red Army officer was standing in the shadows by the fire. There was a revolver in his hand.

'There will be no noise, please,' the man said in German.

Eisler heard the outside door open. He turned. Another two Russians stood in the porch with machine pistols levelled at him. Their coats, like the officer's, reached almost to the ground.

He put a hand on Margaret's shoulder and said: 'Don't be frightened.' But there was fright in his own voice.

Again the Russian said, 'There must be no noise.' He turned to Margaret. 'Sit on the couch.' He waited until she had done so before looking again at Eisler. 'I am Major Yepishev. You are Herr Walter Eisler?'

'Yes.'

'Then you are under arrest and will come with me.'

It was twenty-five years since Eisler had looked into the barrel of a gun with a Slav face behind it.

'The Red Army has no right of arrest in this country,' he said.

'I am arresting you in the name of those who have the right.'

'Whose name?'

Major Yepishev seemed to make a quick decision. He stepped forward with a peevish expression on his sharply-boned face and struck Eisler a swift blow on the shoulder with the barrel of his revolver.

Margaret moaned and half rose from the couch as Eisler sagged to one side with a noisy intake of breath, his face flushing and then fading grey.

'Whose name?' he gasped again.

'I am arresting you in the name of loyal elements of the Deutsche Demokratische Republik.'

For *loyal elements*, Eisler thought, read the names Zetkin and Bahr. Through the pain and the bewilderment a ludicrous notion came to him. Had others been making war while he made love? Had there been a *coup* while he frolicked in the woods with Margaret, making promises of spring? That would make a good footnote in the history books. Was Zetkin forming a new government? The clock on the wall showed the time as only a little after five. Nothing could have changed. Nothing can have changed, he told himself.

His shoulder had gone numb and he could hardly move his right arm. He wondered if he was going to be able to keep from vomiting. He looked at the Russian with queasy curiosity. The man was accoutred as if for a long campaign, with pack, water bottle and steel helmet hung about his square-shaped body. He looked tense and ruthless. When he got his medal and his promotion for this, no doubt the words would be *alert* and *heroic*. Eisler had seen the same man on a thousand posters. He had been every-where and done everything. He had captured Berlin, saved Stalingrad, seized the battleship *Potemkin* and cut a few royal throats at the Winter Palace. He was ageless, indomitable, probably immortal. He would be the first Russian on the moon. Once he had been Eisler's hero.

'You are acting illegally,' Eisler said. 'Where is my bodyguard?'

Major Yepishev looked surprised. He turned ques-tioningly in the direction of the two soldiers. They stood in menacing attitudes as if Eisler was dangerous. None of them spoke.

'Get out of here at once,' Eisler said. He knew the command was ridiculous. What was Margaret thinking of him? She was sitting staring into the fire as if stunned.

'My orders are to take you with me even though you have to be rendered insensible first,' Major Yepishev said.

'Take me where?'

'I have no authority to tell you that.'

Even fear had not completely crushed Eisler's instinct for bargaining. 'I will come with you if the lady is left here in safety.'

Major Yepishev smirked bitterly. 'You politicians can never resist making conditions.'

He stiffened a little as if regretful of the small, unmilitary lapse. 'Fortunately, my orders are to leave the lady here. With a warning.' He turned briskly to Margaret.

'Herr Eisler is coming with us. You will remain here and contact no one.' His expression suggested that this would not have been his way of handling things.

She rose from the couch and grasped wildly at Eisler's arm. 'I'm coming with you. They're not going to take you alone. I'll never see you again.'

'Do as he says, Margaret. I'll be all right.'

Major Yepishev's brow furrowed and he stepped

anxiously forward as if something had just occurred to him, something not covered by his orders and in which he would have to use his initiative.

'Speak only in German or Russian,' he said. With his free hand he pulled Margaret away from Eisler, and then pushed Eisler backwards. 'English is forbidden.' He stood glowering at them while his immense load of equipment thumped back into place against his hard body.

*

Eisler was pushed into an armoured car from which he had no view and driven along what he judged, from the absence of noise or halts, to be open country roads. When he was ordered out all he could see was a wooden hut with a light above the door.

He was put inside and left there. It was dark and cold and smelled of oil. There was no window and although he found a switch it produced no light.

Presently he heard the roar of powerful engines; revving, fading, revving, fading; then a concentrated burst of power which gradually dwindled into the distance. He was on an airfield.

The hut was completely unfurnished. He could either sit on the floor or lean against a wall. For an hour at least he moved, shivering, from one position to the other before he was taken out under a guard of at least twelve soldiers and marched, like a desperate and practised escapee, across more than a half-mile of frosted tarmac. The only language he heard was Russian. The lights of an aircraft showed ahead. As he climbed, blinking, into the brightly lit interior, Major Yepishev's voice said: 'You will sit somewhere over there, please. Any seat will do. Then do not move or ask questions.'

Three hours later the jet landed at Shermetyevo, Moscow, and shortly after eleven o'clock Eisler was seated at a table in the Kremlin facing Kozhnev.

It was a room that he had been in several times before, although Kozhnev had not then been the man at the table. Little had changed. It was not a room in which much change could take place; the green cloth top of the table, the single white light hanging low, the surrounding shadows. The first time he had seen it he had thought of billiards.

Without preliminary, Kozhnev pushed a document across the table and followed it with a pen.

'Sign that,' he said pleasantly, 'and you will be back in the arms of your lady before dawn.'

It was the assured voice that Eisler remembered from the days when they had often sat together until midnight and beyond, in Kharkov, with the plans of dismembered German factories spread in front of them, arranging the next day's work. In Kharkov he had always done what Kozhnev wanted. He had been good at the job, but Kozhnev had been better.

He began to give names to the other faces at the table. Alessoy, Garkov, Malishniev. It was a big night.

He said: 'I protest at this criminal act.' He was surprised at how much conviction he was able to put into the words considering that this was the land of no protest.

'Traitor!' It was Garkov's voice, rutted and broken with over-smoking, like the surface of some remote cart track in his native Ukraine.

Kozhnev glanced sideways. 'We need no unnecessary insults,' he said sharply. He leaned a little further into the light, showing a disappearing hair line and grey puff-balls under his eyes.

You have gone further than me, but worn less well, Eisler thought. The irrelevance of the thought and the bleak little burst of satisfaction that accompanied it, surprised him. The mind, he supposed, must hide its confusion in trivialities.

'Sign, Comrade.' Once it had been: 'We will start digging here, Comrade.' 'We cannot wait for cranes, Comrade. The prisoners will lift the girders.' 'We will abandon this site, Comrade.' Always the decisions had been justified. The work had gone on faster than anyone else could have pushed it. Kozhnev had achieved the same success in all his jobs, including this one. Above all in this one. Here his range was global. He had combined the public relations flair of a Khruschev with a brilliant administrative skill. He had dedicated himself to putting a new glitter on the Soviet world image and had gone about it in ways that had shocked the hardliners, making a series of surprising concessions to the West and to China.

Eisler opened the document in front of him. It was double foolscap-size and folded. The writing on one side was in Russian; on the other, in German. It was a personal declaration in which he repudiated all six points of *Our Socialist Future*. In abysmal language he declared his ideas to have been grossly mistaken and founded in counter-revolutionary inclinations which he now recognised, regretted and promised never to repeat. Some of it was almost laughable but when he reached the references to nervous strain and over-drinking he tore the pages in half and threw them back across the table.

'I would have thought you knew me better than that,' he said.

Kozhnev seemed undismayed. 'This room has witnessed more dramatic renunciations,' he said civilly.

Marshal Malishniev lifted the torn scraps. He was old and his voice was thin and unsoldierly.

'I would ask Comrade Eisler to reconsider,' he said, as if speaking not to Eisler, but to the others. 'It would be the least troublesome way. The repudiation would remain here, known only to those of us who are in this room to-night.' His voice came as if from some windswept

63

extremity of the Steppes. 'You would go home,' he said, looking at Eisler for the first time. 'In a week or two you would let it be known that you feel you have misjudged what is possible.' He raised his shoulders. 'For a while, if you wished it, there could be some gesture to the Press. Perhaps also a more tolerant attitude towards those who wish to go through the Wall. In two or three months the foolishness would be forgotten.'

'And the abject confession?'

'It would only be needed if you failed to keep your promises.'

'I will sign nothing and I will make you no promises. And I demand to be returned to Berlin.'

Garkov said: 'Why do you wish to borrow money from Western Capitalists?'

'So that I can buy oil and coal from them.'

'You can buy oil and coal from us.'

'Yes, but at prices I would be ashamed to charge to an enemy. Those are not negotiators you have sent to me. They are highwaymen.'

'We have overheads in relation to your country which the West does not have,' Garkov said impatiently. 'We maintain twenty divisions for the defence of the DDR.'

There was an obvious answer to that but Eisler, even in his bitterness, felt he would probably be in more need of it later. He said: 'Comrades, if I borrow Western money I can buy Western oil and coal at favourable prices. These are basic commodities which affect the prices of many products. Cheaper oil and coal would allow us to lower production costs in many industries. If our goods are cheaper we can export more of them. The more we export the higher the standard of living for our people. It is good business.'

'Buy! Sell! Business! Wah!' Garkov made a noise as if he was spitting. 'You talk like a London Jew, Comrade.'

'And you act like one, Comrade, plundering us of our produce at wickedly low prices and selling us, almost at gunpoint, goods that you can't dump elsewhere.'

From the far right of the table, where the spread of light was weakest, and the smoke thickest, Oleg Alessoy, Secretary of the International Committee of Governing Parties, spoke.

'I would be interested if Comrade Eisler would explain to us why he is so anxious to expose his Government to the dangers of a Volkskammer Opposition.'

'Because it would make it easier for us to borrow money in the West.' As he saw their expressions he wondered if it was too ingenuous an admission. 'Another reason is that opposition means competition. Where there is competition one has to be vital. An opposition would be good not only for the efficiency of the S E D but for the country.'

'Competition!' Garkov's sour expression turned again to contempt. 'More Jewish talk.' He turned to the men on one side of him and then to those on the other. 'We are in the market place, Comrades. He wants to run his country like a vegetable stall.'

For a moment it looked as if he might leave the table in disgust, but he sank back with folded arms as Malishniev started to speak.

'Another of your strange desires is to have the Red Army vacate its bases in East Germany. Surely this would not be prudent?'

Eisler felt that Malishniev's gaze was less unfriendly than it had been earlier.

'Marshal Malishniev,' he said, 'we freely acknowledge our debt to the Red Army. It is one that we will never be able to repay. Nevertheless, no country likes to feel it has an occupying force on its soil.' He tried to smile despite the dull sickness that filled him. 'It is a matter of national pride. Foreign troops, even the troops of our greatest ally, give us an inferiority complex.' He managed another humorous grimace. 'Perhaps we Germans are a little conceited, but, after all, the war ended in 1945.'

Malishniev's voice seemed to gain strength. 'Allow me to correct you, Comrade. The war did not end in 1945. Only the fighting stopped then. You are in fact still an Occupied Zone. There has never been a Peace Treaty.'

Kozhnev moved a little in his chair and, as if recognising a sign, the others waited for him to speak.

'You are young. You have thirty years of power ahead of you,' Kozhnev said. 'You are throwing it all away.' He looked genuinely sad.

'If I cannot do what I believe to be right with power, then I do not see much point in having it.'

'You took an oath to the Cause.'

'I took another oath to seventeen million Germans.'

Kozhnev lit a cigarette without offering one across the table. 'I want to ask you one question. Have you faced up to the fact that the logical outcome of your intentions will be the collapse of the German People's Democracy?'

Eisler's shoulder stabbed pain as he leaned across the table, looking earnestly at each of them in turn. 'Comrades, I implore you to see that the outcome will not be a collapse of the people's democracy, but its glorification. I do not seek to cast out Communism, only to adapt it to the needs of my country. And, with respect, my country is not your country. My people were not starving peasants whose loyalty could be bought for the price of two or three half-reasonable meals a day. We Germans were part of the mightiest and most advanced country in Europe, debauched for a decade and more, it is true, by the Hitler criminals, but with a technical and cultural heritage unknown beyond the Oder. Again, with respect, my people expect more than your people because they have always had more. All I want to do is give them what

66

they expect and deserve. To do this I must break the shackles of useless dogmatism. But I promise that what I do will be done within the framework of Socialism.'

He sank back exhausted. Garkov's pot-holed voice came trundling out of the shadows.

'So, Comrade Eisler, as an ideologue you set yourself above Marx and Lenin?'

Eisler shivered. The stones of the Kremlin would bleed before a mind like Garkov's would let in light. In despair, he began addressing his answer to Kozhnev.

'The principles of Marxism-Leninism are constantly being adapted, even here in the Soviet Union. What does not change will die.'

His voice rose angrily as he turned again to Garkov. 'I can tell you that Marx and Lenin would not be standing to-day on the decaying platform that you still occupy.'

They stared at him with emotionless faces.

'You must know,' Kozhnev said quietly, 'that if this aberration of your Praesidium is endorsed by the Central Committee then we would be forced to consider taking very drastic action.'

He did not need to draw a picture. Columns of armour were already grinding through Eisler's head. In the end, he supposed, he would have to compromise. But not yet, he thought fiercely. Not yet. The longer he waited, the further he took them, the more he would get away with. All at once, all he wanted was Margaret. They could have their Wall and their censorship and everything else if only he could have her. Something wet and hot fell on the back of his clenched hand. It was a tear. The men on the other side of the table ignored it. What was a tear?

'I will go to the people with this,' he said threateningly.

'I advise you not to do that.' Kozhnev's voice was as controlled as ever. 'Already you have the diplomatic world seething. Think well before you unleash more primitive forces that neither you nor we might be able to control. That could be a desperate situation.'

'It is surely a desperate situation when the Soviet Union seems to be saying it is prepared to violate my country's sovereignty.'

Garkov made his spitting noise again. 'The only sovereignty you have, Comrade, comes out of the barrel of a gun – and a Red Army gun at that. Your sovereignty is as spurious as your theories. As Marshal Malishniev has already reminded you, the so-called Deutsche Demo-kratische Republik is in fact the Soviet Occupied Zone of Germany.' He choked a little, either in excitement or on his cigarette. 'We have made you and we can break you,' he finished in a splutter.

The brutal words turned Eisler sick again. He turned appealingly to Kozhnev. 'I cannot talk under such horrifying threats.'

Kozhnev smiled slightly. 'Comrade Garkov is a forceful speaker.' The smile slipped away as if it had come between him and something he wanted to say. 'Your wish to demolish the Wall worries me militarily as well as econo-mically. It has become a bulwark against Federal Ger-many. It is now your early warning against attack.'

'Can anyone seriously imagine any circumstances in which West Germany would ever attack us? It would plunge Europe and the world into war.'

'You Germans have done that twice already this century.' Kozhnev's voice had gone bitter. There was no smile now.

'West Germany has a treaty of non-aggression with you,' Eisler said.

'The treaty of August, 1970, has given us a respite in Europe and allowed us to concentrate on China,' Kozhnev said. 'But it was possible only because of the dream of one man – Chancellor Brandt. It changed nothing in the hearts of the German people and it was opposed by the German war-machine. One day Chancellor Brandt will go. The German people will go on. The German war-machine will go on.' He paused. 'Anyway, even if your programme did not include the dismantling of the Wall we would still be gravely opposed to it.' He pushed his chair back and stood with his head lost in the upper darkness. The light shone brightly on his open jacket and on the brass buttons of his red vest. 'I think the picture I want to leave with you, Comrade, is of those twenty Red Army divisions encamped within your frontiers.'

When they had gone, the guards took Eisler out of the warm conference room and led him along corridors and down stairs to a cell built into one of the outer walls of the Kremlin. He had seen these places before in a conducted tour of the fortress. Beads of ice sparkled on the undressed stone. He sat shivering and then lapsed into a sleepy daze. He was wakened by the guards. They walked him into a courtyard and put him into an armoured car which drove off so abruptly that he struck his head on a steel stanchion. He felt blood dribbling down his face.

The armoured car stopped on an airfield which he saw was not Shermetyevo. The aircraft this time was an Antonov troop carrier. Major Yepishev was more remote than ever. Again Eisler dozed on the hard seat. It was still dark when the Antonov landed. Another armoured car. Another long drive. When they stopped, Major Yepishev said: 'This is your destination.'

Eisler stepped from the vehicle in an aching daze. Almost before he had steadied himself the armoured car shot away with the driver making a bad job of the gears.

As he looked about in the darkness, Eisler saw that he was alone and standing on a country road at its junction with an unpaved, tree-lined lane. It was the lane leading to the house near Potsdam where Margaret lived.

Chapter Ten

There was a light above the door and he noticed for the first time that the brass knocker was shaped like a Swastika, an incongruous relic of the former ideology. There was a sound behind him.

He turned and saw a gun and behind it Comrade Zander – black-jowled, red-eyed but alert and springy looking, almost taller. As they recognised each other the gun dropped and Comrade Zander's expression turned to one of almost tearful relief.

Eisler said: 'Is Mrs Sloane all right?'

As he spoke, the door rattled open and Margaret threw herself into his arms.

In the house Eisler turned accusingly to the bodyguard. 'Where were you?'

Comrade Zander came to attention. 'I decided to take the car for petrol. On the way, it stopped twice. At the garage they said it was a fault in the electric petrol pump. I had to go back to Berlin to get a replacement. When I came back you were . . . gone.'

Eisler sank on to the couch. Exhaustion was flooding through him. 'It's perhaps just as well,' he said wearily. 'They might have put a bullet into you.'

Comrade Zander's expression suggested that a bullet wouldn't have been so bad.

'Have you made a report?'

'I wouldn't let him,' Margaret said. 'I made him do what they said I had to do. We've been sitting here all night drinking coffee.'

'Then don't report it,' Eisler said. 'I'll attend to that

myself.' He had a strong wish that the kidnapping should not become public knowledge. Certain people would inevitably get to know, but that was very different from a full-scale public furore. One day it would all come out, but not yet.

Apart from the political enormity of his kidnapping, the revelation of which might start a chain reaction of events beyond his control, Eisler's sense of dignity was deeply offended. He felt the Russians had succeeded in degrading him. He was sick with disillusionment. The whole episode might have been an exercise in contempt rather than intimidation. Kozhnev seemed to be saying to him – *See, little man, we can do with you as we wish. We can take you out of your own country when we feel like it and no one can stop us. If you had never been seen again no one would have known what had happened to you. As it is with you, so it is with your silly little republic. We will crush every one of you if you make us. What do seventeen million Germans matter to us? We lost twenty million Russians fighting you Germans in the war.*

For a while, Margaret was another problem. First he had to calm and reassure her then, as she recovered from the shock, thwart her instincts as a journalist.

'They're thugs,' she said. 'They should be exposed. That's the one thing that hurts them, having their sins paraded in public. They can sew up their own newspapers so tightly that it pains them all the more to know the news is being broadcast to the rest of the world.'

He was filled with a sudden fear for her safety. 'No, not until I say so. Apart from the fact that it suits me to hide this meantime, your position here is delicate enough, as you keep telling me.'

It was only later that he saw the irony of his attitude, set alongside his plan to ungag the Press. Fortunately, Margaret did not see it then, either.

'They wouldn't know it came from me,' she protested.

'I could go to West Berlin and spread the word from there. I could confuse it even further by not giving it to an American paper. Ten minutes in the Springer building is all it would need.'

'No.'

'You're wrong, Walter. If the world knew about this there would be such a rumpus that the Russians would find it ten times as difficult, from a public relations point of view, to try anything on you later.'

He knew there was sense in this but it couldn't be done without his plans being prematurely publicised. The vital need for him was to stick to the due – if laborious – processes of Party ratification. He must have the Party with him. The Party was the seat of his strength. Without that he would be useless. Exposing the Russians – if he really wanted to expose the Russians – was a minor matter.

*

On Monday morning Eisler went back to Berlin.

Margaret was at the door of the house as Comrade Zander put the luggage in the boot of the car. When he had locked the boot he walked towards her with an embarrassed smile.

'I had better say good-bye.' He hesitated and then added with shy intensity, 'I hope you will be very happy.'

Margaret smiled. 'I hope so, too, but why so solemn, why good-bye?'

'When Comrade Bahr hears . . .' He turned from her to Eisler with a fatalistic spreading of his hands.

There was something about the way his head was tilted, as if away from his troubles, that made Eisler want to comfort him. He said: 'I don't suppose Comrade Bahr even knows your name.'

'He will get to know it now.'

Eisler took another uneasy look at him. He had enough

troubles without taking on a bodyguard's worries as well. But he had shown himself to be discreet. The next one might be a nuisance.

He said: 'We will say it happened when I sent you into Potsdam for cigarettes.'

He would have stuck to Comrade Zander's petrol pump story but he was certain that an examination of the car would show that the old pump was still there.

Comrade Zander made a sound of gratitude but his face was still forlorn. Standing there in front of the old house, his shadow short and trim in the white winter sunlight, he suggested to Eisler's imagination a porcelain figure from the early Meissen period.

The wide-brimmed black hat was missing and so were the buckled shoes but Eisler could still picture him perched on a woman's knee, his little hands steadying a candle holder or a receptacle for flowers.

But you're not a Meissen figure, he reminded himself. And you were on some romp of your own when you should have been here seeing that nothing happened to me. After a moment he smiled wryly at the self-importance of the thought.

Chapter Eleven

Politicians have an awesome hold on life. Prime Ministers and Presidents will sack entire Governments in order to retain office. It is news when a politician resigns and as a class they have probably the lowest suicide rate on earth. They, even more than soldiers, understand the need to attack unexpectedly and from the least likely quarter. One of their weapons is confusion. Having managed to secure secrecy, Eisler's next inclination was to baffle his enemies.

Next morning he sent for Karl Zetkin, who arrived looking immaculate but, Eisler thought, vaguely furtive. This was a good start. What you are expecting at the very least, Karl, he thought, is an awkward question or two. You are possibly even prepared to be accused outright of conspiring with a foreign power. You will have your answers well rehearsed. Let me confound you, then, with something that you are not expecting.

Eisler held out his cigarettes and said casually: 'Karl, I thought we might discuss your next job.'

'My next job?'

'Yes. After all, when we get this reform programme going there will be less for you to do. The intellectuals can start talking and writing their heads off. Your job will diminish. I thought that for a man of your capabilities and experience . . .'

He stopped as if noticing for the first time the expression on Zetkin's face, managing to convey that it was only a thought, and that if Zetkin would be quite happy in a position of reduced responsibility, then why should he care.

74

He sat in silence, enjoying the sight of Zetkin floundering.

'I hadn't thought things had quite reached that stage yet,' Zetkin said.

It was the first time Eisler had heard words come to Zetkin with such obvious effort. All the elaborate pose had slipped. The Dresden factory girls might not have been so attracted to him in this revealing moment.

'The moment may not be here, but it is coming,' Eisler said. Let him pass that on to Moscow. 'We must plan ahead. Spring is our time. It won't be long. It is almost Christmas now.'

On the other side of the Wall, he knew, coloured lights hung on trees and Rudolf Braun, who had been over to discuss joint fire precautions, had come back talking enviously of the shop windows in the Ku-damm.

'The Central Committee has still to accept your proposals,' Zetkin said huffily.

'You do not have to instruct me in S E D procedure, Karl. In any case, that is not what I brought you here to discuss. We were talking about your future.'

Zetkin, he guessed, saw his future – his near future – as the Soviet-bolstered Chief of State of the Deutsche Demokratische Republik. The handsomest man on the Praesidium was all set to become the handsomest man on the world stage of Communism, perfumed by Old Spice or whoever it was, tailored like an English Tory.

'I am mapping out some possible changes of responsibility,' he said. 'I wondered if you had any preferences.'

Zetkin had recovered slightly. 'If you could give me a little time to think.' He was absent-mindedly examining the creases of his narrow-cut trousers.

'Of course.' Eisler waved negligently to his empty desk, then grimaced as the simple movement sent pain shooting through his injured shoulder. 'I happened to have a blank fifteen minutes. I thought it would be useful to mention this to you. Think about it.'

As Zetkin began to look relieved at what seemed to be the end of the discussion Eisler added in an off-hand way; 'I've been wondering, actually, how you would take to farming, but . . .' he raised his hand '. . . don't tell me just now. I have another appointment.'

A pleasing picture came to him of a demoralised Zetkin wading miserably through the quagmires of Saxony or Mecklenburg, trying to show interest in the collectivised potato harvest.

This was the kind of childish yet inescapable man-oeuvring that cut time from every day. Never had it seemed more worthwhile. The effect he'd had on Zetkin so cheered him that he couldn't stop just yet. 'Oh, and another thing,' he said recklessly. 'I don't need Party ratification to take down the Wall. The Wall is adminis-tration, not policy.'

He walked to the door and opened it. Zetkin left looking very tame.

*

In the afternoon Eisler called unannounced at Julius Bahr's office. Bahr had another man with him. They were hunched over some magazines spread about on a table by the window. When he saw Eisler, Bahr started to dis-miss the other man.

'Finish what you are doing, first,' Eisler said. 'I am in no particular hurry.'

Bahr's head moved jerkily as he indicated the scattering of magazines. 'It is of no great importance,' he said. 'Just more filth from the West. Some American culture.' As Eisler stepped forward, Bahr said: 'Pornography smuggled in from the other side. We will have to find the source and stop it.'

As if guiding Eisler, his yellowing eyes moved over the lurid covers of the magazines, over the big bare thighs and preposterous breasts, from one sniggering title to another – *Don't Stop Or I'll Scream. No Wonder She Felt Weak In The Mornings.*

Eisler turned a few pages of one of the magazines and said: 'Why did she feel weak in the mornings?' He supposed that out there, in the world beyond reach of the Party's good intentions, there would be people eager for this filth. He remembered Margaret saying that the Communist vision of culture was a yawn, but this, he thought with a twinge of sad superiority, this is degradation.

Bahr was saying in a flustered way: 'You heard the First Secretary's question, Heinrich. Why did she feel weak in the mornings?' He turned apologetically to Eisler. 'You understand, Walter . . . I have not read them myself. They have just arrived.'

'I didn't really expect . . .'

But Heinrich, with a slight smirk, was already addressing Bahr's cracked black shoes. 'Her boy friend had an identical twin,' he said. He looked up hopefully but Bahr's expression had not changed. It was still the face of a man trying to recall something – something pleasant – and failing.

'What?' Bahr said.

Heinrich rubbed his pink hands together and then put them neatly at his sides. 'There were two of them, you see. They were doubles. When one gets up – to go to the toilet or have another fix, or anything – the other one gets in beside her. She doesn't know the difference.'

Eisler watched and listened in slightly astonished distaste. Heinrich had the appearance of a balding schoolboy for whom, already, human endeavour could produce no surprises.

Bahr was frowning. 'Fix?'

'Drugs. They all take them in these American stories. They are all junkies.'

'What are junkies, please?'

'Addicts.'

Eisler interrupted. 'Julius . . . maybe it would be better, after all, if you did adjourn this for the moment.'

Bahr made a quick signal to Heinrich to leave the room and to take his pornographic magazines with him.

Eisler said: 'I had no idea your work held such variety.'

'It's just another of the hundred-and-one things we get thrown at us in this department,' Bahr said with a self-satisfied wave of his hands.

'Yes, you are very versatile, Julius.' Kidnapping one day, erotica the next, he thought. He walked to the window. 'My own business is also rather unusual but vastly more important.' He swung round. 'I want to invoke Paragraph Nine.'

Bahr stopped in the act of climbing on to his high chair. 'Paragraph Nine?'

'Yes. Paragraph Nine.'

It was the section of the Ordinance for the Security of the People's Republic which provided for special investigations to be undertaken against members of the Praesidium. Eisler did not know when it had last been invoked. Perhaps never. Doubtless some disgruntled or incensed people had tried to express themselves through Paragraph Nine but it was hedged about with so many dis-incentives that to set the apparatus in motion was almost impossible.

Would-be crusaders – or trouble makers – were confronted with the solemn preliminary rigmarole of signing a declaration that their motives were totally pure and that they harboured no personal animosity against the person whom they would later be permitted to name. Next, they were handed an excerpt from Paragraph Nine which dealt with the penalties that could be inflicted on persons attempting to misuse the law by laying spiteful or mischievous charges. This was followed by a period of reflective isolation in a waiting room. Only the exceedingly determined or foolhardy went further. In the silence of the cell-like waiting room suspicions were inclined to falter and fall dead. Irrefutable evidence was suddenly seen to be hollow, transparent and generally ramshackle. Only after a citizen had passed these tests could an examining official even listen to what he had to say. Even then, the last and greatest hurdle had yet to come, for the decision whether or not to initiate an investigation rested solely with the Minister of State Security.

'Paragraph Nine.' Bahr's groan suggested that he had enough worries without this. He retreated a little from his chair as if it had turned out to be too high for him, as if the aura that enshrined the two words had left him dazed and blinded. 'Is something wrong?'

Eisler looked at him impatiently. 'Naturally.'

'But what is it?'

'I have reason to believe that the criminal act of taking me to Moscow was carried out with the knowledge and probably even at the instigation of certain members of the Praesidium.'

Bahr's sick face began to writhe horribly. 'That is a fantastic suggestion. It can't be true.'

'How do you know? Until this moment, have you even considered such a possibility?'

'Of course not.'

'Then choose your words more carefully, please.'

Bahr seemed to have abandoned his attempt to sit. He stood by his chair, one hand resting weakly on the seat, as if for support, like a child just learning to walk.

Eisler had looked up the procedure. Now he said:

79

'Where are the forms?' He looked about irritably as if they should have been lying somewhere handy.

'Forms?'

'There is a procedure. Certain forms have to be completed. I assumed you knew about these things.' He looked accusing. 'It is your department.'

'Of course, of course.' Bahr lifted the telephone and went into a long and excited explanation of what he wanted. At last he put the telephone down. 'Please tell me now what is happening.' In his weakness it was possible to see another figure; the cruel child protecting itself by sanctioning practices which a stronger person could not have faced.

Eisler frowned. 'I think people in our position should obey the law to the letter. It would be very wrong of me to tell you anything before the forms have been signed as prescribed in Paragraph Nine.'

After this rebuke Bahr said no more. They waited practically in silence for another five minutes, Bahr fidgeting and occasionally mumbling.

When the forms came and had been solemnly read and signed, Eisler said: 'Now you can question me.'

He almost laughed at the bafflement on Bahr's face. 'But what have you to tell me, Walter?'

'Very well. Last night I had a telephone call from a man who knew that I had been taken to Moscow. He said it had been arranged by a group of three in the Praesidium and that the leader of that group is Karl Zetkin.'

He didn't care what he said. All he wanted to do was spread some consternation. The hoarseness in Bahr's voice told him that he was succeeding.

'Did he . . . did he give the names of the others?'

Eisler let him wait a little. 'No,' he said at last. 'No other names.'

'And who was this man on the telephone?'

'He would not tell me.'

Bahr's shoulders rose and fell. Relief spread thinly across his grey-skinned face. He tugged at the lobe of one of his big ears. 'But Walter . . . an anonymous telephone call . . .' He made it sound ridiculous.

Eisler looked at him coldly. 'It is not so long ago since you came to me with an anonymous letter complaining of my friendship with Mrs Sloane.'

Bahr's expression said oh-now-let's-be-fair.

'All that was required of Mrs Sloane was that she should agree to answer a few formal questions. There was no imputation against her. But . . . Paragraph Nine . . . is it right that we should come to an affair of such gravity through the words of an unknown man?' He was managing now to give a reasonable impersonation of a fair-minded Minister of State Security concerned only to see the right thing being done.

Eisler appeared to be affected by Bahr's moderation. 'You think I'm being hasty?'

'Who can speak of haste in relation to what happened to you?' A smile wavered round Bahr's face, a little at a time, as if the territory was unfamiliar and not very pleasant. 'Naturally, you are angry. You have been told certain things. You can hardly be expected to ignore them. You want some action taken.' He vaulted suddenly on to his high chair and sat there for a moment looking like a circus performer who expects applause for a difficult trick well done. 'In your position I would also want action.'

'Paragraph Nine is the complete answer,' Eisler said roughly.

'Perhaps, but it leaves you little room for manoeuvre, no room to withdraw.'

'I don't want to withdraw. I want to attack. If Zetkin is mixed up in this I want him exposed.'

Bahr looked across at the window table as if wishing he was still involved only with a few pornographic junkies.

'But if Zetkin has done nothing. Your position would be very awkward. I could act much more discreetly if you left me to proceed as I thought best.'

In the end Eisler allowed himself to be persuaded. He had done what he had come to do. Bahr would have to look as if he was doing something about Zetkin. It would be worrying for both of them. As he walked to his car he regretted that such deviousness had been forced on him. What he wanted was a sunrise but more than ever he saw now what a lot of murk would first have to be swept away.

Chapter Twelve

The Wall and its attendant tank-traps, water-filled ditches and electrified fences winds through what should be the heart of Berlin for a distance of just over thirty miles, creating a grey zone of dusty, moon-like deadness on either side. No one builds near it. Under its shadow, things crumble. Houses which existed before the Wall have been empty for years, their outer doors closed with nine-inch nails, their windows blanked with brick. Beyond the city, the Wall goes on its ugly way for another seventy miles, sealing off with concrete and barbed wire the border between West Berlin and the surrounding East German countryside.

At three o'clock on the morning of 15th December Red Army troop carriers arrived simultaneously at every one of the Wall's command posts. Within half an hour, every East German guard had a Russian beside him. There were no orders to cover such a situation. Here and there scuffles developed. A few Russians were bitten by patrol dogs. Somewhere out in Thuringia two shots were fired and an East German sergeant died. He was the only casualty.

As the attack began, Eisler was wakened to take a telephone call from Moscow. There was no conversation. Kozhnev spoke what was obviously a prepared statement.

'I wanted to let you know,' Kozhnev said, 'that the Red Army has at this moment started certain peaceful manoeuvres in your country. These manoeuvres are concentrated at this moment mainly in the area of the Wall. Later in the day they are scheduled to spread to other areas. It is unfortunately not possible for me to tell you at this moment how they might develop or when they will end. I need hardly say that they are necessary to the proper exercise of our responsibility as the Occupying Force in your Zone, and have been occasioned by a build-up of the Imperialist forces adjacent to the Zonal Border.'

The cynicism of it filled Eisler with rage, but as he started to protest, Kozhnev said: 'There is nothing you can do. Go back to sleep.' The contempt was terrible. There was a click as the call ended.

By morning, Russian tanks were standing in Alexander-Platz, Marx-Engels-Platz, Karl Marx Allee and Unter den Linden. Armoured cars toured the city at ten miles an hour with their aerials up and the observers relaying messages to an unknown headquarters.

Eisler did what he had to do.

GREAT RED ARMY EXERCISE, said *Neues Deutschland*. MASSIVE SHOW OF SOVIET STRENGTH TO IMPERIALIST WARMONGERS. And so the message went out in every radio and television news bulletin. But despite the official explanations, people began to walk the city instead of going to work. Groups formed at street corners and at cafe tables. At home, they tuned in to Western television and radio and heard different interpretations of the manoeuvres.

By noon, KOZHNEV TURNS THE HEAT ON EISLER was one of the headlines flashing across the Wall from the elevated free news signboard in West Berlin. EISLER'S SOCIALIST FUTURE GIVES MOSCOW THE JITTERS.

In mid-afternoon a truck load of Volkspolizei raced down Unter den Linden to disperse the silent crowd which had gathered outside the Soviet Embassy.

By now, there were Soviet tanks in the streets of Rostock, Magdeburg, Leipzig, Weimar and Dresden. The tanks rumbled in and then stopped as if from mechanical failure, the crews eventually climbing out and crouching on the cold superstructure in glum groups. The rebellion of 1953 had been crushed by Soviet tanks and the relationship between the people and the Red Army had been bad ever since. Now, a street with a tank in it was avoided almost as if by decree.

Behind every report that was handed to him, Eisler saw the faces of Kozhnev, Garkov and Malishniev as they had looked at him across the green-topped Kremlin table. How far were they prepared to go? He exhausted himself trying to see the possible moves through their minds. They would do nothing yet, he was certain, that could be branded as a blatant act of aggression. It was too soon for that. They would want to negotiate and they were putting the pressure on so that they might negotiate from the maximum strength.

If they crushed him, they would want to do so from behind a façade of moral principles, responding, if possible, to something – anything – that could be made to sound like a cry from the people.

Here was Zetkin's chance. If he had the courage to get up now and denounce Eisler and show that he had another two or three quislings behind him, the Russians would have the excuse they needed. If Zetkin appealed for Russian help to save the country for the workers he could be in power by to-morrow. Would he feel strong enough? Several times, out of curiosity, Eisler attempted to contact Zetkin. He was not in his office. Eisler did not doubt that he would be with the Russians, either at the embassy or in one of their barracks.

After talking with those whom he could contact, Eisler called an emergency meeting of the Praesidium for that evening and an extraordinary meeting of the Central Committee for the following evening. He wanted *Our Socialist Future* to become Party policy without another day's delay. Then he tried to telephone Margaret. She was not at the house and had gone, the caretaker said, to Potsdam as usual. She had probably left without listening to the news or buying a newspaper. Lickspittles was her word for the journalists who worked for these propaganda services. For a while he was tormented by the thought that they might try to get at him through her. He almost sent Comrade Zander to fetch her and get her to the other side of the Wall before evening. Then, he rejected the idea as premature and melodramatic, telling himself that if it did come to a Russian take-over, Margaret would, as an American, be able to leave as she wished with the other foreign visitors who were scattered about the country. She had broken no law.

Early in the morning he had sent formal Notes both to the Soviet Embassy and direct to Moscow, protesting at the alarming nature of the manoeuvres and deploring the opportunity they would give to Western propagandists. Now he toured the city to see the situation for himself. He came back exhausted with anger and apprehension, half wondering if there would be a Soviet guard on his own office.

To his dismay, about a hundred people were waiting in the cold street. As they saw his car they came uncertainly forward, saying nothing, just watching.

He had to gather himself before stepping on to the pavement, forcing an expression of calm confidence. He gave a few smiles and waves and then hurried inside after a breathless messenger had come running out with the whispered word to an aide that they had been alerted to a call coming from Moscow.

It was Kozhnev with an invitation to Eisler to attend an emergency Warsaw Pact meeting in Sofia two days later. 'It is to discuss the relationship of each Socialist state with the others,' Kozhnev said.

'My place is here,' Eisler said bluntly. 'If my attendance is desirable then the meeting will have to be held in Berlin.'

Kozhnev's voice was sarcastic but unsurprised. 'Very well, I will come to you. All the other busy men will leave their work and come to you.'

'It will make no difference to any of you except the Bulgarians,' Eisler said.

'No matter,' Kozhnev said, as if making a concession. 'It will give me a chance to see the manoeuvres. I hope they are causing you no trouble.'

Eisler's temper flared. 'How much longer have we to be subjected to this dangerous display of force?' he asked angrily. 'If it continues I cannot guarantee the continued good nature of the people.'

'You are not being asked to guarantee anything.'

'Already one of our Border troops has been killed.'

'Suppress the fact.'

'I will not suppress it.'

'Then bury him with full honours,' Kozhnev said with sudden viciousness, 'and send the bill to us.'

'It is intolerable. How can I explain such things to the people? They already guess that these are no ordinary manoeuvres.'

'I regret the death.' Kozhnev sounded as if he meant it. 'It is a blot on an otherwise flawless exercise. A small blot. Nevertheless, I will send you an official apology and we will compensate the next-of-kin.'

And some day, Eisler thought, you will probably shed similar tears at my funeral.

Chapter Thirteen

Rain was smearing across West Berlin in a foggy grey cloud through which the traffic hissed slowly, headlights flicking nervously at junctions and an occasional horn crying out in surprise.

In Finckensteinallee the lights had been on all day.

By mid-afternoon Woolcott had collected almost as many reports on the situation as Eisler.

'It looks,' he said contentedly, 'as if everything is going to be all right now.'

'I'm glad you think so,' Derby said. 'It looks a bloody sight worse to me now that the Russians are on the Wall.'

'No.' Woolcott shook his head tolerantly. 'When I began to get worried was when the Russians whipped Eisler off to Moscow and then let him go again. However, these manoeuvres, this flexing of the bear-like muscles, has brightened the picture. This is more like the Russians that we all know and love.'

'You think they'll give Eisler the heave?'

Woolcott came away from the window. 'Either that or Eisler toes the line,' he said brightly. 'Either way, we can all start breathing again. The Russians will soon come off the Wall and disappear back into the scrub.'

'You know, I'm sorry for Eisler,' Derby said in a puzzled way. 'His aims are a hundred per cent laudable and yet – East or West – he doesn't seem to have a friend in the world.'

'You're forgetting,' Woolcott said, 'Eisler has one very good friend. We must not lose sight of her.'

Derby smiled as if he had been told a smutty story.

'Margaret Sloane?'

'Interesting, isn't it?'

'She's just a newspaper writer. I told you I met her in Vietnam.'

'I don't know,' Woolcott said dreamily. 'Here and there I feel I can read between the lines. Some day the girl might be shown to have been very much a factor. He might be doing all this to impress her, you know. Perhaps without knowing that's why he's doing it.'

Derby made a scoffing noise.

'You think that impossible, Ramsden?' Woolcott's face suggested that there were some great loves that only a few men – he among them – could know about; that it only needed the right woman to come along and he would be perfectly capable of doing the same as Eisler.

'I don't think it very likely.'

'Well, the whole situation shows such a lack of judgment that we must seek an unlikely explanation. I'm pretty certain Eisler is suffering from some sort of mental upheaval. The poor chap is besotted with love, that's my theory. He is being destroyed by it. His judgment is gone. No doubt he wants to make everybody happy, but it wouldn't take much for us all to end up dead instead.'

He stopped momentarily to see how Derby was taking the theory.

'He's a middle-aged bachelor and he's fallen for this girl like a youngster of eighteen. I'll bet he's tip-toeing through the tulips while I go cold at nights wondering about the peace of Europe.'

As Derby opened his mouth Woolcott said with a quick smile: 'Oh, and another thing.'

Derby waited.

'You'll be glad to know that the President agrees with me about the dangers of this situation.'

Derby laughed. 'You've been talking to the President?'

Woolcott's lips twitched a little, perhaps to indicate that he understood Derby's sense of humour. 'He's told all the Nato governments what his views are.' Woolcott opened a folder and began to read from it:

'The Eisler manifesto is one of the biggest threats to peace that has arisen in Europe for many years. The peace of Europe has been preserved by the maintenance of a power balance between East and West. The defection of such a vital satellite as East Germany would upset this balance. As I see it, the Russians have no option but to crush Eisler, by force if necessary. It is my belief that we must sadly recognise this as realistic and inevitable. And if it happens we must remain inactive. We must make the propaganda noises that the world will expect us to make, but no more. Neither by word nor deed should Eisler be encouraged. He could be fatal for the peace of the world.'

Woolcott looked pensive. 'That's the essence of what the President believes, Ramsden, and I happen to know that the British Prime Minister agrees with him. These are men of vision.'

He rose from his desk as if in a trance. He moved to the window and looked down to the street. 'Things have been so quiet recently that I'd almost forgotten this was an occupied city.' The way he was talking into the curtain gave his voice a muffled quality. 'You could walk about all day and maybe never see a man in military uniform. Now, all of a sudden, the place is crawling with American and British troops.'

'Don't forget the Froggies,' Derby said.

'Vive la France,' Woolcott replied without a smile. He went back to his desk by a circuitous route that took him halfway round the room, touching things as he went as if feeling his way in the dark. He lowered himself into his chair and looked at his watch. 'In an hour or two things will be even worse.' His voice was sombre.

'Worse?'

Woolcott gave a lugubrious nod. 'There's going to be a big Allied build-up in case the Russians start getting any ideas about this side of the Wall while they're cleaning Eisler out. To-night we start flying in extra troops.'

Chapter Fourteen

The rain had turned to snow. Here and there, Russian tank crews lit fires in the streets and crouched round them trying to boil water or heat food.

Comrade Zander passed a snow-covered troop carrier parked outside Humboldt University and crunched on with lowered head in the direction of Friedrichstrasse railway station. He had written down the description of the girl that Fräulein Kopf had given him and he took a look at it again in the light from an H O bookshop window.

Before moving on he looked to see if there was any new poetry on display but all he saw was the same old stuff about Party heroes, broken up with a few novels about factory workers and great dramas of the land.

It was a tense night for Comrade Zander. He felt that he might be walking towards the most important moment of his life; a moment when, according to the poets, time could stand still, bells ring, sunshine flood the night. *And I will love thee still, my dear,* Comrade Zander said softly to himself, *till a' the seas gang dry.*

His eyes moistened as he remembered his mother holding his hand as someone in a kilt sang these words at a reception in the local hall a year or two after the war. It had been the voice of a comrade from Scotland, choking a little from all the vodka they had given him. *And I will come again, my love, tho' t'were ten thousand mile.* It was the haunting sweetness of the words that had turned Comrade Zander to the works of Robert Burns.

He approached the appointed place at the stated time

with the stealth of a defector keeping what might be his last rendezvous before going over the Wall. The meeting place was the doorway of a privately owned dress shop in a turning near the station. There was a clearance sale on and even from here he could see the crushed and dated look of the unrepeatable bargains. He stopped, still on the opposite side of the street, and looked across at the female Fräulein Kopf visualised as his wife.

She was in her late twenties and quite pretty, he decided, in an ample sort of way that was all in proportion and would not be thought of as fat for a few years yet. In the glow of the shop lights her hair looked almost silver and newly set. But she was like millions of other women. He hadn't joined a marriage bureau for this he thought resentfully. He hadn't asked for time off and sneaked down here in the middle of a national emergency for this. He wanted something special. Fräulein Kopf would have to do better than this. He could get this sort of thing for himself.

He considered walking boldly past the girl. But suddenly he was devoid of boldness. Instead, he stepped off the pavement and wandered away into the snow, limping a little with fright and faint nausea; one of life's permanent walking wounded.

Chapter Fifteen

By eight o'clock that night seventeen men and two women had been shot trying to get over the Wall. Fifteen were dead and the others seriously wounded. It was as if every unhappy citizen had read somewhere in the dry, swirling snow that to-night was the last chance for freedom, that if things had been bad before, soon they were going to be worse.

There was nothing organised about any of the attempts. No one was armed. None of them came charging at the checkpoint barriers in armour-plated buses or banded together and ensured that, by numbers alone, some were bound to succeed. It was more a mass madness. At widely separated points the pathetic human shapes – the desperate, the sick, the great unorganised who had little hope of succeeding, who hadn't thought about it for more than a few hours – were picked up by the searchlights and efficiently gunned down into the snow. Some of them seemed almost to be waiting for the bullets rather than seriously trying to escape.

Next morning's Western newspapers were to call it MASSACRE ON THE WALL and by that time the dead would total sixty-seven and the injured fifteen. It was as if the darkness had been charged with a message of despair to which, as the night wore on, more and more people became receptive.

The first suggestions of carnage reached Eisler as he prepared to leave his office for the meeting of the Praesidium. Earlier, he had spoken to Margaret on the telephone. He had asked her to come in from Potsdam and go to his flat, where he would join her as soon as he could. The sound of her voice had steadied him and after the call he had gone back to work with still an hour to go before the meeting.

His first impulse, as the terrible reports came in, was to telephone the commander of the Border troops and order a cease fire. What did it matter if a few hundred or even a few thousand people clambered over into West Berlin? But did he have the power to issue such an order? And if he did have the power, it certainly extended no further than the DDR's own forces. He had no way of stopping the Russians from firing.

*

In the past he had attended some sombre meetings of the Praesidium. To-night the atmosphere was leaden. Some of the members looked weary and dispirited, others might have been through harrowing physical experiences.

Otto Schacht lived almost on top of the Wall in a block of flats reserved for high Party members. He told in a numb voice of how he had gone to his window in time to see a girl trapped in a huge blast of searchlight power. Everything about the girl was startlingly clear. Her hair was black and held high on her head by a curved comb. Schacht said it looked as if she had just been to a hairdresser. She was wearing what were probably her best clothes, very high heels and a short fur coat, and she was carrying a light-blue suitcase. She stood for a long time in the light as if not knowing what to do next. Then she began to move unsteadily towards the Wall, walking as if she did not want to get snow inside her shoes. Voices shouted to her to stop, but she kept going. So far there had been no shots.

The girl had picked a stretch where the guards were either badly trained, sympathetic or chicken-hearted.

Eventually three shots were fired but they all missed. Schacht thought they had probably been aimed wide by reluctant men. There was a silence of perhaps ten seconds before another single shot came. This time the girl stopped, looking round as if surprised. She lifted a hand towards her head and then fell heavily on her side. As she hit the ground her suitcase burst open and a jumble of delicately coloured fabrics tumbled into the merciless white of the illuminated snow. Schacht had spent the next two or three minutes being sick.

'I didn't know it was like that,' he said in the same dead voice as he had told the story, looking round them as if he didn't care what they thought of him. He had thick lips and an inclination to blubber when things went against him. 'I never thought of them as just girls, just ordinary people,' he said stupidly.

'The law says they are enemies of the State, whatever they look like,' Karl Zetkin said softly. 'The country is betrayed just as much if it is a girl of nineteen or a key factory worker of forty.' A matchstick that he had been twiddling with snapped between his fingers. He looked at the pieces thoughtfully before dropping them into an ashtray.

Adolf Anbricht pulled out an old-fashioned pocket watch and glanced at it like a bus driver checking his schedule. He still had to get back to Karl Marx Stadt to-night.

'What is happening out there must make us all feel sick,' Anbricht said. 'Including Comrade Zetkin, I'm sure. But unless there is something we can do about it – and we all know there is nothing – let us not be diverted from the real purpose of this meeting.'

Eisler gave him an apprehensive nod, for what in effect they were here for was to pronounce judgment on him. Were they still coming with him, now that the Russians had shown what might happen, when people were being mown down on the Wall by the dozen? Their expressions told him nothing except that they had all been unnerved by the events of the day. The creeping death in Julius Bahr's dusty face seemed to have quickened. Again Eisler wondered if the man was suffering from some secret pain to which he would not admit. For once, Bahr was making no effort to give the illusion of extra height. To-night he seemed to have another pre-occupation. He was sitting on the edge of his chair, bent forward a little, with his stubby arms resting on the table. He looked more shrunken than ever.

Eisler searched Zetkin for similar signs of strain. Zetkin was sitting well back from the table in his usual attitude of disassociation. Was he a little less well groomed than usual? Or was the dishevelment in Eisler's mind?

Only Albert Behrens was missing. A message had come in to say that he was in Stralsund and could not be back in time for the meeting. One less supporter, Eisler thought. One less vote.

He started by telling them that the rumours of his forced trip to Moscow were true. He told them as much as he could remember of the document that Kozhnev had wanted him to sign.

They listened with shocked expressions and kept interrupting with questions.

'I have not retreated a single step,' Eisler ended. 'And with your support I will stand firmly to the programme mapped out in *Our Socialist Future*. What I want to-night is a reaffirmation of our intentions so that I can tell Kozhnev that we are unshaken by his threats, and so that to-morrow's meeting of the Central Committee will be in no doubt of our desire to carry through the programme which we have asked them to endorse.'

As he sat down there came from his left a sound that

could have been made in protest, or perhaps only in doubt.

'You think this is realistic? Are any of us likely to have any kind of future if this goes on?'

It was Paul Mauser, the fat, spiky-haired Party boss from Rostock. He looked along the table. 'I have driven here to-day, comrades, through a land once again giving every appearance of being occupied by the Red Army. Is anyone going to tell me that it is not?'

Zetkin threw him a cigarette and Mauser frowned a little as he read the English brand name.

'I warned Walter that this is what would happen,' Zetkin said. His face was expressionless and it was impossible to tell whether he was accusing Eisler or commiserating with him. He was waiting, Eisler supposed, for the others to reveal themselves. Then he could judge his possible strength. A pretender with no supporters would be unacceptable to Moscow. Come to us heavy-laden and we will give you power was the way Moscow looked at things.

'It is an outrageous attempt at intimidation,' Eisler said. 'But can we know for certain if it is any more than that?' Perhaps if he could convince them he could convince himself.

So far, he still could not judge what impression he had made. 'We are being treated as headstrong children who must be shown the whip, but will the whip ever be used with so many neighbours looking on?'

'It has been used before,' Mauser said gloomily. He looked, with his crumpled collar and ash-marked jacket, like a servant whose job demanded that he should try to look neat, but whose nature was all against it.

'That was before Kozhnev's time.'

Mauser snorted loudly. 'After what he's done so far do you think he'll suddenly stop?'

'He might lose his nerve before we lose ours. He has

set in motion a terrible display of strength, but he cannot be happy about it. The danger for Kozhnev is that the situation might get out of control. The day after to-morrow he will be even less happy. He is coming here in another attempt to browbeat me. He will fail.'

He was astonished at the assertion. It suggested strength and courage, but he was weak and probably foolish. Under the talk and the posturing he was afraid. What he wanted above all was to get home to Margaret.

Otto Schacht loosened his tie and collar. He looked pale but mumbled something about being warm.

'Ministers and members of the Praesidium previously without bodyguards will now have them,' Julius Bahr suddenly announced, straightening at the table and looking about as if someone had asked him what he was doing about it all.

'Well, I hope mine is a bit huskier than that midget Walter has,' Anbricht said.

Eisler smiled. 'The smaller they are, the less obtrusive.'

A faint flush had come into Bahr's cheeks. Perhaps he still had a little blood left. His voice was angry.

'Has Comrade Anbricht never been to any of our displays in the Volkspolizei gymnasium in Hans Beimler Strasse? He would soon learn there how little mere height matters.' He was speaking not just for himself, or Comrade Zander, but for small men everywhere.

Eisler turned consolingly in Bahr's direction but before he could say anything Zetkin started to speak. He was still the same aloof figure, his chair still pushed two or three feet out from the table. He was wearing a pink shirt with a dark-blue suit and he was like no other man in the room. What was he, Eisler wondered. Cool cynic? Many-splendoured careerist? Stalin worshipper? There was silence, as in a theatre just before the act with top-billing comes on. This was the decider. Some of them would

99

undoubtedly take their lead from Zetkin. Should he listen? He had learned, by the swift evolutionary process that comes to all politicians, how not to listen. It was the only way to survive the torrent of talk. Almost immediately something in Zetkin's expression made Eisler switch on.

'Attempts have been made to humiliate and demoralise our First Secretary,' Zetkin was saying. 'What happened to him yesterday could happen to any of us to-morrow. Despite suggestions that have been made to the contrary . . .' he smiled faintly in Eisler's direction '. . . I am a patriot. I still feel that Walter wants to go too far too fast. For me, however, and I imagine for most of us, this is no longer the issue. The issue is, do we control our own affairs, mapping out our course as we see it, or is this to be done for us in Moscow? There can be only one answer. They've left us with no choice but to stand up to them.'

Eisler sat pouring water, fumbling with a cigarette packet. It couldn't be true.

Schacht left his seat and went over to the window as if he no longer cared what any of them were saying. 'It is far too hot in here,' he said as he passed Eisler.

And yet it must be true, Eisler thought. Not even Zetkin could be this devious. He could never redeem himself from this patriotic stance. Was he sincere, then, or was this the result of Paragraph Nine working in his system? Had he decided to wait and fight some other day? If so, it was a miscalculation. He would never get a better day than this.

There was a screeching noise as the window shot open. A few flakes of snow drifted in on the sharp night air. Schacht leaned out as if looking for something. Then he turned a little and said: 'Come and listen to this.'

They gathered at the window and took it in turn to put

their heads out. The snow had almost stopped and there was no wind. Two or three streets away a fire flickered on the pavement, showing the dark outline of a Russian tank. What Schacht wanted them to listen to was the throb of aeroplane engines as the Allied troop carriers circled over West Berlin waiting their turn to land.

Chapter Sixteen

Margaret had the television tuned to West Berlin. The programmes were being constantly interrupted to give news of the deaths on the Wall and of the beginning of the Allied military build-up.

When Eisler came in she was at a table near the window rearranging some books and brass ornaments. It was a pose, assumed, he imagined, when she heard his key in the lock, a studious denial of the situation for fear of what it might do to them.

With two fingers she tested the earth round a group of plants in a trough. She said: 'Do you ever remember to water these?'

Her face, he thought, like the perfume she wore and which now filled the bachelor room, had been created, as on a canvas, by the rejection of everything gross and ordinary. It was the kind of face that might have been produced by a long line of despairing artists.

'Not very often,' he said. He felt desperately ashamed that she should see his country like this, the wounds gaping and the people in pain. He supposed that she knew this and in her way, with this nonsense about plants, was trying to spare him.

'The poor things are parched,' she said.

'The woman who comes in is supposed to look after them.'

'Women who come in never do half what they're supposed to do. At least, in America they don't.'

'You usually do,' he said with a cheerful ambiguity that surprised him.

She made a creditable effort to be coquettish. 'I'm different,' she said. 'I'm in love with my work.'

It was as far as she could go with the game. As he searched for another smart answer she switched the television off and came quickly across the room.

'Walter, you look terrible. It's only a couple of days, but you've lost weight and you're so pale.'

He kissed her and then stood holding her tightly, his eyes closed, his voice choking in his throat. 'There's been so much going on.'

She pulled back as if to see him more clearly. 'You're shaking like a leaf.'

'Am I?'

'You'll have a nervous breakdown.'

'I'll be all right. I've been up since about three o'clock this morning.'

He saw that she had set a table for supper. It was the only sign of normal activity that he could remember seeing that day.

'They'll kill you, one way or another,' she said wildly. 'I know they will. You're a menace to them.'

'I have given my life to them.' He looked baffled. 'I can't really believe it's all happening. Once I get away from my office and all the talk it seems like something I've imagined.'

'It's real, all right.' Her fingers dug into his arms. 'How much more are you going to take, Walter? You should get out while you can.'

He looked at her with a puzzled expression, as if searching her words for some meaning other than the obvious one. 'Leave my job?'

'Your job . . . the country . . . the whole rotten gang of them. Why not? You can't go on believing in Communism after this.'

His hands performed awkward movements of protest. 'But this isn't Communism, Margaret. This is gangsterism.'

'It's always been gangsterism. Can't you see? In any emergency the guns come out. It's the only answer they've got. But it's an unbeatable answer. You can't win.'

Her last words were the most wounding he had ever heard.

'They would be delighted to let you go,' she said. 'It would solve everything for them. And for us.'

'There are enough refugees in the world without me joining them,' he said. 'I wouldn't be very good at it.'

'You wouldn't really have to give up anything. I mean, not money, or comfort. I can think of three or four newspaper or magazine groups who would pay a fortune for your story.' She smiled. 'You would be the richest refugee in the world.'

'Rich?' As a child, he had always wanted to be rich. His heroes had all been princes or merchants.

'Yes. A million dollars wouldn't be an exaggeration.'

'I would be able to join all the exiled kings and queens in Portugal,' he said. 'The million-dollar refugee. It's a lovely dream.'

'But it needn't be a dream, darling.' Wet rivulets glistened on her cheeks. 'If you don't do what they tell you, or leave, something terrible will happen. You're rocking the whole Communist boat.'

'Garkov is the most reactionary,' he said, as if determined not to abandon hope. 'Perhaps if it was only Kozhnev . . .'

She shook her head. 'You're too forgiving. They are all accustomed to the use of violence. And Kozhnev is probably mad. He's certainly schizophrenic.'

He looked surprised and then waved a limp, dissenting hand. 'He's a brilliant man.'

'Perhaps. But I was reading one of his speeches yesterday in an old newspaper that I found lining a kitchen drawer. In it, he actually spoke of love, the love that Mother Russia has for her children. It was disgusting, and I think what disgusted me most was a suspicion that he really believes it. He made me think of an inquisitor protesting his love for the man he is about to burn.'

Eisler thought: I understand the attitude better than you ever could, Margaret, because there was a time when I came close to it myself.

He said: 'What would people think of me if I ran away?'

'I don't know what other people would think, and I don't care, but I would love you for it because I'd know then that we had a life ahead of us.'

The irony of it washed through him. 'It's odd that you should be so anxious for me to throw it all up, Margaret. Do you know what some of them think about you?'

She waited while he sorted out the words.

'Old Albert Behrens says that you'll get the blame of putting me up to all this. The suggestion is that I'm under your evil influence.'

She made a scoffing sound.

'*They will say it was her hand which planted these seeds in your heart.* Those were Albert's words. It's a pity he can't hear you now.'

'Don't leave it too late, Walter,' she said in a calmer voice. 'Please don't leave it too late.'

He crossed to the window. The troop carriers were still circling overhead and it was snowing heavily again, the big dry flakes sticking momentarily to the glass and then falling away. Down the street, the skeleton of another new Government building had been draped and softened into a shape of mysterious woolly beauty, the scaffolding standing round it like a fluffy Christmas packing that had started to burst at the seams.

'I'm going to fight them,' he said.

She sighed. 'How can one man fight the Soviet Union?'

'It isn't one man,' he said stubbornly. 'I've got the Praesidium with me. To-morrow the Central Committee will back us.'

'You can have God Almighty and the whole chorus of holy angels on your side,' she said in a queer burst of mock Irish accent, 'and it won't make a bit of difference if the Russians decide to take over.'

He put his mouth against the warm, scented hair at her temple. He felt a pulse beat against his lips. To-night, she seemed fragile and breakable. Her eyes were tired and he could see a few strands of grey in her hair. He wondered who, or what, had put them there so soon and regretted that they belonged to a previous life that he had not shared.

'Wouldn't you fight for something you believed in?' he said.

'I suppose I might,' she said reluctantly. 'If there was something I believed in.'

The answer shocked him. It suggested a cynical desolation too great for him to accept. He put his hands on her shoulders and began to shake her in an uncontrollable surge of anger.

'Why are you so bitter, Margaret? You have no right. You have everything. Out there in the snow people are dying for something that you take for granted. All they want is to get to the other side of a wall. Some of them might not even really want to get to the other side, they only want the *right* to go there. You can cross whenever you feel like it. You don't understand what it means not to be able to. I want to give these people a little hope, but all over this country to-night hope is dying.'

106

His voice shuddered to a standstill. His hands dropped limply from her shoulders. He could see by her face that he had been hurting her. They stood looking at each other in dismay. This is what she had been trying to avoid, and although it was impossible she had been right to try.

Chapter Seventeen

Comrade Zander watched the double oak doors of the conference room close on Eisler and the eighty-three members of the Central Committee. The next three hours were his own. They could get on in there with deciding the future of the country. Out here, he had his own future to consider.

The slushy streets were busier than on a normal week-day morning, for despite the exhortations in *Neues Deutschland* and on television, few people had gone to work. They walked slowly about the city as if they could not settle, grey-faced, anxious, cold from lack of sleep. Comrade Zander was one of the few people in Berlin – east or west – who had spent the night soundly.

He walked carefully to avoid the heaps of half-melted snow. Shoes weren't what they used to be. To-day, there was perhaps less sign of the Russians, but all the main squares and crossings still had Red Army tanks or ar-moured cars parked on them; waiting like ambulances at a football match.

He had to walk a long way before he could find a taxi and when he told the driver where he wanted to go he got a curt shake of the head in the best fraternal tradition.

'What's wrong?'

'Too near the Wall. The Vopos have warned us to keep clear.' Obviously, he did not think much of Comrade Zander. He was a local and locals did not tip these days. You had to depend on Western Capitalists for that, or on subsidised Arabs.

'Then take me as near as you can.'

A quarter of a mile from where he wanted to go the taxi stopped and the driver went through the prescribed formality of working out the fare on the pad that they all carried. Comrade Zander completed his journey to the marriage bureau with a walk through streets in which many of the shops were closed and in which only the primeval, yellow-snouted buses seemed at home.

An old poster commemorating the fiftieth anniversary of the Revolution flapped in his face from a grey wall. Perhaps Fräulein Kopf wouldn't be there. He seemed to be the only person in East Berlin pursuing the normal course of life; if a visit to a marriage bureau could be considered normal.

Comrade Zander felt totally unconnected with the crisis or with the tragedy of the night before. He had seen it all on television and this morning the figure of sixty-seven dead had flashed in his eyes from the elevated news signboard across the Wall. It caused him neither anger, shame nor despair and he would have been just as indifferent if he had read that sixty-seven people had escaped. He had never met them. He didn't know their names. For him they did not exist. Comrade Zander could not cope with life in terms of abstracts. For him, all ideas had to be embodied. He was ready to die in his job not for the Cause but simply for Eisler's protection. The training had been directed at making him see Eisler as the embodiment of the Cause but Comrade Zander saw him only as Walter Eisler. It wouldn't have made any difference to him if it had been Hitler.

He opened the yellow door and stepped into the bare wooden corridor almost thirty minutes before his appointed time. He knocked at the bureau door and when there was no reply he tried the handle. The door opened and he went in.

The gas fire was hissing unsteadily as if the pressure was so low that the ancient apparatus was having a struggle to keep going. Fräulein Kopf was not in the room.

He closed the door and stood for a few seconds experiencing the vague excitement that comes with unauthorised entry. There was a diary on the desk showing two blank pages and a tear-off calendar that hadn't been adjusted for almost a week. The faint scent in the room might have come from flowers but there were no flowers. He guessed it was one of the unexotic perfumes that the system made available.

He stepped lightly round the desk wondering where he should pry first. He tried the door which he thought had a cupboard behind it. It opened. In the light from a low-hanging bulb he saw a pulled-back carpet and an open trap. He stood quite still for a few moments and then quietly crossed the room. The space below the floor was in darkness.

Comrade Zander hitched up his wide trousers, lay flat on the floor and put his head into the hole. In all directions there was darkness. He took a torch from his pocket and lowered it into the cavity, at first cupping the light in his hand and then gradually letting the beam shine freely. Immediately below him there was a small cellar reached by a flight of wooden steps. The cellar space was almost entirely taken up by gaping sacks filled with earth and rubble. The remaining clear space took the form of a passageway between the sacks. The passage led to a hole in a brick wall.

Comrade Zander listened. There was no sound. He went down the steps and walked to the hole in the wall. It was the entrance to a short, recently-hewn tunnel which opened out into a cellar similar to the one directly beneath the marriage bureau. Here, the floor was also filled with sacks of debris and in the far wall there was another hole.

He went no further. He climbed back up the wooden steps and out through the door of the bureau into the grimy corridor. He was shocked, not at the existence of the tunnel, but at Fräulein Kopf's carelessness in leaving the door unlocked.

From the corridor a public stair led to the floors above. He began to climb it. Most of the apartments were used now as offices but some were still residential. He could smell food and hear radio or television voices. If he knocked at some of these doors what panic there would be to switch off the forbidden stations.

On the top landing there was a filthy window set into a discoloured wall. When Comrade Zander stood at it, on the tips of his toes, he might, against the light, have been a convict looking from his cell. He studied the scene in detail, judging distances and directions, picturing the view in relation to what he had found under Fräulein Kopf's floorboards.

Beneath the window the ground stretched away to the edge of the death strip in an ugly avalanche of half-cleared bomb sites and bricked-up buildings. This was the desolation that guarded the Wall. Beyond the marriage bureau, life stopped for all but the guards and the trained dogs.

Most of the buildings were old tenements from which the occupants had been evacuated when the Wall was built. One day they would be demolished but there were more public places to be beautified first and there wasn't enough cosmetic to cover everything.

Comrade Zander had been reared in an apartment block of this type. He could still remember the cellars that he had played in as a child. Originally, they had been intended for storage, but by his day damp and neglect had made them useless. He remembered battered washing coppers covered in a hideous green skin that showed even through the dust, and heaps of woodwormed furniture. The cellar of each tenement was separated from the next by only a thin partition wall of brick. In most of these brick walls holes had been knocked when mains water and gas or electricity had been led into the old buildings, so that in some places a whole maze of streets was linked by a series of subterranean caverns. Exploring these musty warrens had been an adventure. It had been possible to enter a cellar in one street and by going through the holes in the walls not resurface for perhaps half a mile.

The boy Zander had at one time peopled these dark places with murderers, ghosts and treasure hunters. It was odd to think of Fräulein Kopf down there in her sunglasses and white blouse.

He admired the set-up. Tunnelling had never been a favourite method of escape. The starting-off points close to the Wall were regularly patrolled and the surface monitored with sound detectors. To find a safe starting point meant embarking on an almost impossibly long tunnel. Whoever was behind Fräulein Kopf's tunnel had been led to the idea by a childhood memory. Once the space under the marriage bureau had been linked to the existing cellar system hardly any excavating would be needed; perhaps a little for purposes of direction. Possibly the old cellars went right under the Wall, since the barrier was totally unnatural and had no basis in anything but man's wretchedness.

When he went downstairs and into the bureau again Fräulein Kopf was at her desk. The flame at the wheezing gas fire was very low. The room was cold and so was Fräulein Kopf's voice as she said:

'Well, what happened, Freddi?'

He was grateful for the blankness of her sunglasses. 'You mean, about last night?'

'Eva telephoned me. She waited for ages. It wasn't fair of you standing her up.'

'I'm sorry,' he said, thinking that to look at her you would swear her only concern was for other people's love lives.

'Especially last night, with all that terrible business on the Wall. Some streets were full of soldiers. It wasn't a night for a girl to be wandering about on her own.'

He sighed for his lack of gallantry.

'Something could have happened to her.'

He tried to think of a few words in his own defence, but she didn't give him time.

'There's absolutely no use me making an appointment for you if you don't keep it.'

'Oh, I kept it, Gerda, but she didn't look . . .' his head shook a little with the effort of deciding what it was the girl hadn't looked like '. . . didn't look . . . like what I want.'

'But you can't go by appearances.'

You can say that again, he thought, as he looked away from her to the door that led to West Berlin.

'I picked her because I thought you would have a lot in common.'

'Tell her I'm sorry. I'll write and apologise.'

If she kept going on at him he'd ask her how her tunnel was getting on. He was the best judge of what he liked. He was certain the girl would have been hopeless for him. Maybe it would always be hopeless. Maybe there wasn't a girl for him. The trouble he had was in talking to them. The things he knew most about weren't spoken of. Comrade Zander knew all the places in the human body where pressure, skilfully applied, could produce silent, instant death. He was not ashamed of these skills. They were the only qualifications he had. But they were hardly the substance of small talk. An irrelevant memory came to him of a television show in which two ferocious Asiatics, with their heads shaved except for greasy knots standing in the middle, had demonstrated karate techniques. Comrade Zander had found it hilarious. He had been convulsed by their old-fashioned expressions of menace, the elaborate ritual and the ludicrous noises that they made with their mouths before each blow. Compared to them, he was a glittering instrument of the electronic age, programmed to dispense bare-handed destruction with unemotional economy.

They both turned in their chairs and stared as the gas fire panted convulsively, gulped a few times and went out with an exhausted plop.

'The pressure,' Comrade Zander said, welcoming the diversion.

'Yes.' She nodded. 'And the pipes.'

'The pipes?'

'The supply pipes. They are very old. I meant to get them cleaned when I came here.'

It seemed a good opening. 'You haven't been here long, then, Gerda?'

'Only since October,' she said. 'I've a lot of things I still want to do.' She looked convincingly at the dis-tempered walls as if one day they would be papered.

'Where was the bureau before you came here?'

'It wasn't anywhere,' she said with a faint smile. 'I had a baby linen shop before this.'

He closed his eyes, trying in a dazed way to see her among the rompers, the rattles and the waterproof pants. 'You are not trained to this work then?'

She laughed as if he had made a joke. 'There is no training for this work, Freddi. I told you I was guided here.'

Guided, he thought, by two or three men with picks and shovels. 'Oh, yes,' he said, 'by the Loving Hand.'

Her glasses tilted sharply for a moment as if she was trying to see more deeply into him. She relaxed with a thin smile. 'I thought that here I could help people.'

Yes, but to do what? Tie the matrimonial knot or cast off the shackles of the fraternal heaven? So far, she probably hadn't told him a lie. He was getting to like Gerda Kopf more and more.

'Freddi . . .' She seemed suddenly to be thinking of something else. 'Do you write poetry yourself, Freddi, or just read it?'

He hesitated. What was this knack she had of reaching through all the muffling to his deeply buried heart? It unsettled him every time he came here and yet, to her, he wanted to talk.

'I once wrote a poem,' he said shyly, 'but it was no use.'

'What was it about?'

His face twisted in a puzzled way, as if it had never occurred to him before that even a poem must be about something, even a poem written by him.

'I don't know,' he said. 'Nothing.' He realised with alarm that he already had it half way out of his wallet.

'Is that it? You kept it, then. Please read it to me, Freddi.'

He thought her teeth were very white and the hollow of her throat soft and warm-looking in the glow of the tinted table light. He imagined pearls lying there, or a white flower.

'I couldn't,' he said. 'It's no use. You would only laugh.'

She looked hurt. 'Is that the impression you have of me? You must know I wouldn't laugh.'

'But you wouldn't like it.'

'Go on, Freddi. Read it. I'll tell you truthfully what I think of it.'

The scrap of paper had been folded and unfolded many

115

times. At two or three of the folds it was in holes. Comrade Zander's voice was hoarse as he read from the disintegrating sheet.

The cooing dove does gently fill the night, and sadly fills my heart with thoughts of years ago. For many times that dove and I have stood and watched and mourned. For whom? We did not know.

He stopped and looked across the desk at her but the dark of her glasses told him nothing. He started to read again;

She in her tree and I below, together, older than we seemed, we watched and mourned. Why? Oh, now we know. But then, those years ago, each in our separate ways, we felt this strange elusive thing. But neither knew just then for whom. Or why. Not then. But now, Oh now we know.

Fräulein Kopf was silent for a few seconds and then, seeming just to notice that the reading was over, she said: 'It's beautiful, Freddi, but so sad.'

'No,' Comrade Zander said. 'It's terrible. I've always been meaning to throw it away.'

'Oh, you mustn't do that. You must leave it with me so that I can copy it. Would that be all right?'

He gave a baffled nod. Her interest in him couldn't be real.

As he rose to go she said, almost anxiously: 'What is it you know, Freddi?'

Comrade Zander looked again at the door behind her and thought: *More than you think, Gerda.* 'Know?' he said. 'Know?'

'Yes. The last line. It keeps going round in my head. *But now, Oh now we know.* What is it you know now?'

'It's nothing,' he said.

'Is it something sad? Or secret? You have such sad eyes.'

116

He thought she was going to take his hand. She was so near that he could feel her warmth. At the time, the poem must have meant something, but not now, especially with Fräulein Kopf standing so close to him. 'It's nothing,' he said again as he backed out of the room. 'It's only a poem.'

Chapter Eighteen

'You have company to-day, Mrs Sloane,' the attendant said as he turned the key in the lock of the fireproof door. He smiled. 'But you are still our favourite customer.'

Four times a day he unlocked this door for her, twice to let her in, twice to let her out, and always he had ready some little gallantry.

He was in his sixties, with thinning grey hair and a straight back that must have shrunk a little if the faded green uniform had ever fitted him. On her first day, she had decided that he was a dispossessed landowner and although the few remarks that he had made about his past had tended to discredit this theory, it was how she still saw him.

'Is it the bearded doctor from Vienna again?' she asked. 'I liked him.'

'No.' He patted his cheek with one thin hand in a mild gesture of despair. 'They would not renew his visa. He wrote to the Custodian only last week telling him that he could not come back. He was a nice man.' He shook his head wonderingly as he pushed the big door inwards. 'No, this is a countryman of your own.'

As usual, he was reluctant to let her go. As she stepped inside, he said: 'As the morning passed we thought that perhaps to-day you were not coming, Mrs Sloane. Is it very bad in Berlin?'

'Very bad,' she said in a low voice. 'That's why I'm so late. The train services are disrupted.' As in all such places the inclination was to speak in a whisper, usually out of consideration for others; but here she felt it had more to do with the dead than with the living. The people she had come to know here were not alive. From this place, ghosts would go with her and they would never leave her again; Wiesenthal, Morgenthaler, Goldschmidt and many others from the terrible drama of the Final Solution. In a way, it was an appropriate place in which to have met them; soundproof, secure, sealed-off, it could have been a Gestapo torture chamber, and probably had been during the war.

'Is it true about the deaths on the Wall?'

'I'm afraid it is.' She felt there was more she should have been able to say. It didn't seem much of an epitaph for sixty-seven people.

The attendant rubbed the palms of his hands together like a nervous man praying and in the underground still-ness they made a papery sound. 'One day it will all end,' he said as if making a promise to someone not present, but in touch.

If he really believed that, then he had more faith than she had. She remembered Eisler's angry outburst at her bitterness. Perhaps he was right. This poor man could never have known a time of real peace in Germany and yet he still had hope that it would come. He had grown up in the Kaiser's war and progressed through the heartbreak of the Weimar Republic and the black Hitler nightmare to the empty abyss of a Communist old age.

'Yes, one day,' she said, as if she, too, was a believer.

The attendant moved a little as if he realised that soon he must let her go. 'I will be sixty-five years old in one year and eight months,' he said.

It was a significant age. It had replaced the twenty-first birthday as a symbol. At twenty-one, the key of the door. At sixty-five, the key of the Wall. At that age, they were allowed to go. They were past working.

The State did not need them. For women, it was sixty.

'Will you go to the West?'

'I know no one over there now. They have all gone, the people I knew. What could I do? How would I live?' He bent to the handle and got ready to pull the door shut. 'Same time for lunch, Mrs Sloane?'

'Yes,' she said, resisting the temptation to give him something, a packet of cigarettes, a dollar note, anything. 'One o'clock.'

The documents she had been working on yesterday were still stacked with her notebook on the small white wood table that she had used since her first day here. There were no windows but somehow this part of the vault had always seemed brighter than any other.

It was almost noon and she had no inclination to work. Eisler had left the flat early to prepare for the meeting of the Central Committee and she had come here to escape from the empty rooms and the agonised streets of Berlin.

Despite the air conditioning the place smelled of old paper. It was the atmosphere, she supposed, that most aptly characterised her working life. In a score of cities she had sat in places like this taking notes, plodding through the records of other people's pain.

The documents, bound in black, filled five long lines of grey metal shelving. Between these sombre covers were the secret diaries unearthed at Buchenwald, Ravensbruck, and other death-camps of the East Zone, written in the wavering hand of doomed men and women; the business-like log books and reports of camp commandants, doctors and research scientists; the sworn testimonies of those who had survived; if they had survived; sometimes the dead had been luckier.

Sometimes she cried a little as she came on the mementoes that some of them had hidden; a button that looked as if it might have come from a party dress; a brittle photograph of a child, so cracked and brown that it was difficult to tell if it was a boy or a girl. There was a message scribbled on a scrap of label from a disinfectant can, giving the name and number of a guard who continually ill-treated prisoners.

On the far side of the room, hidden by the shelving, sat the other student of horror. She could hear the creak of table or chair and the occasional sound of foot-steps as the man quietly replaced or collected a volume. Was he another writer? War Crimes investigator? An anguished soul trying to lay a family ghost? She did not see him until the attendant came to let them out.

It was Ramsden Derby.

At the sound of the door opening he appeared round the end of a bookcase. He was wearing a long black coat and fleece-lined ankle boots, and he carried his Russian-style hat like a furry handbag. As he smiled, Margaret realised that this was the only expression of cheer she had seen in this room.

She climbed the stairs quickly and then stopped in the street to let him catch up with her.

'My name's Derby,' he said softly. 'Ramsden Derby. I heard the old fellow call you Mrs Sloane.'

The air was still and the sky very blue. For another two or three hours it would be almost springlike but when the sun set there would be a quick freeze.

Derby looked both ways along the wide street. 'Can you recommend a place to eat? I don't know Potsdam.'

'At this time of year there's really only the Kloster-keller.'

'Is that where you go?'

'Yes.'

'Would it be all right if I joined you?'

Without waiting for an answer he began looking about as if for a taxi.

'It isn't far,' Margaret said. 'I always walk.'

The main dining-room was crowded but the friendly, fair-haired waiter who was picking up English from her gave a smiling salute and led them upstairs to where another few tables were set in what might have been a minstrel gallery.

'This is cosy,' Derby said cheerfully. The walls appeared to be of undressed brick. He rubbed a smooth hand across them. 'I wonder what secrets this place has heard?'

'Plenty, I should think,' Margaret said, wondering what secrets it was going to hear now.

He fingered his hair as if to make sure it was still covering the bare patches. 'In this country you can make a remark like that without it sounding too fanciful.'

She held her cigarettes out. 'How do you think it compares with Vietnam?'

He shook his head to the cigarettes and smiled nervously. 'You do remember me, then. I thought you might have forgotten.' He lifted the wine list. 'I wonder what the Russian champagne is like?'

She made a face. 'Twice as bad as American.'

'Should we stick to Moselle?'

'I'll stick to a bottle of Berlin Pilsner.'

'Oh, no. This is on expenses.'

'No, thank you. I've got work to do this afternoon. Wine at lunch-time makes me sleepy.'

When the waiter had taken their orders Derby said: 'Anyway, Mrs Sloane, I don't have to tell you that we haven't met again by chance.'

'I had come to that conclusion.'

His uncertain smile wavered again for a moment. 'But this time it is entirely friendly.'

She looked at the beamed ceiling. 'Is it?'

He stretched out in his chair as if trying to look at ease. Her hand swished angrily over the red-and-white checked tablecloth. 'You were a menace to me in Saigon.'

Derby looked surprised. 'That was nearly seven years ago. You were a bright kid prying into things that could have been embarrassing to the US. I was told to warn you off. The Ambassador was getting worried. I thought you would have forgotten me.' He grinned. 'Or at any rate, forgiven me. It's so long ago.'

'I'll bet you haven't changed.' She made it vaguely insulting.

He looked at her with what might have been admiration. 'You certainly haven't. You're right in the thick of things again.'

She resented the implied compliment. 'Day to day news isn't my line at the moment. I'm researching for a book.'

'I'm told the old instinct never dies.'

'Maybe not, but I'm sitting this one out.'

'It might be the biggest story of your life.'

'I'm sure it's being well covered.'

Derby looked furtive and worried again. 'Not the bit about you and Eisler,' he said. He leaned back from the table as if afraid that she might try to hit him.

He had improved, Margaret thought, since Vietnam, but not by very much. She said: 'That's a name I never talk about.'

'It's a name that everybody else is talking about.' Derby's expression had become slightly frightening in its intensity. 'He's tinkering with the peace of Europe.'

'He's working for the freedom of seventeen million East Germans,' she said angrily.

'The temperature in this part of the world wasn't too bad until a month or so ago, Mrs Sloane. Now it's gone pretty damned cold. I didn't sleep last night for the noise of troop carriers flying into Templehof.'

'It's got nothing to do with us,' she said. 'It's between East Germany and Russia.'

123

He leaned forward, his fingers splayed on the table. 'We're all in it, Mrs Sloane.'

'And what does the CIA imagine I can do?'

He held his hand up. 'This time it's not the CIA.'

'I don't care who you're working for. What do you think I can do about it?'

'I don't know. That's not my worry. My job is simply to make contact.'

'All right,' she said. 'You've made contact but if you don't change the subject I'll be breaking contact. I don't feel very hungry now, anyway.'

'You're a loyal American, aren't you?'

'Oh, please,' she said, making an expression of exaggerated pain. 'Not that.'

'All right. We just want to keep in touch. We want you to know that we're around, just on the other side of the Wall. We'd like you to come over and have a talk with us.'

'What about?'

'I've told you. I don't know.' It was too big an admission. 'I'm not quite sure.' He hunched himself forward, smiling strongly. 'Look. You're a friend of Eisler's. We're bound to be interested in you. We like to keep close to things. This could be a big break for us.' Us? It was a small, homely word but he had a sudden, uneasy hope that it represented something big, something bigger at any rate than just . . . Woolcott.

'You must be mad if you think I could talk him out of his programme, or anything like that. I wouldn't even try. Not for the CIA, the NSA, the DIA, the SIS, NATO, Congress or the President himself. And you can go back and tell them that.'

He looked depressed. 'I told you we only want to keep in touch. The Russians will soon talk him out of his programme.'

'They might not.'

'Well, somebody will have to, Mrs Sloane. Somebody will bloody well have to.'

Derby sat back breathlessly in his chair, oddly alarmed at the intense feeling he had been able to put into Woolcott's brief. It was almost as if Woolcott was able to . . . able to . . . The waiter appeared and Derby signalled gratefully for the bill.

When they came out Margaret walked him to where he would catch a tramcar to the railway station. The sun had gone and the tree behind the tram stop creaked in a rising wind. Derby sneezed and put on his furry hat. It didn't suit his round face.

'At least remember this address,' he said. 'Number Twenty-five Wipperstrasse. I live there. It's the best place to get me.'

'I don't think I'll be wanting you, Mr Derby.'

'You might. It's easy to get to. It's right in the centre of West Berlin, near the zoo. Will you remember that?'

'I'll never forget it,' she said as she put her hand out to stop the tram for him. 'It's so appropriate.'

Chapter Nineteen

During the night a Soviet arms store at Greiffenberg was raided. A band of men dressed in Red Army uniforms bludgeoned two sentries and escaped with almost a hundred rifles and more than fifty thousand rounds of ammunition.

It was the morning of Eisler's meeting with Kozhnev and there could have been no worse start to it.

The Central Committee had remained in session until well after midnight and had ended with a unanimous decision in favour of the reforms proposed in *Our Socialist Future*. Eisler's last comforting thought before falling asleep was that he had behind him a united party. No longer could the situation be misrepresented as a wilful fight of his own for a private dream. Now it was official policy, adopted by men who could not all be romantic dreamers or rash egotists. They had known the solemnity of their decision and its possible consequences and they had dispersed into the tense darkness of the city like soldiers from a battle briefing. In the last dramatic hour of the meeting man after man had resigned the Soviet whip and pledged total support for the reforms.

Now, the strength that Eisler had drawn from them began to disperse as he read the report of the raid on the arms dump. How long, he wondered, before the first bloody confrontation in the streets between Russian troops and German civilians? The provocative Russian manoeuvres had provided every militant extremist in the country with an excuse for violent action. This raid would be an inspiration to other groups. THE GUERRILLAS OF

GREIFFENBERG. The words materialised in his head in sinister black Gothic type. Soon, he thought, there will be the mimeographed news sheets, followed by a rash of 'free' radio stations. It was one of the freedoms that he wanted; but not yet. It could only inflame the Russians. He felt weak and panic-stricken. In desperation he lifted another report and then let it fall. On the Wall, another seventeen men and women had died. In a way, he had killed them, bringing his score in two nights to eighty-four.

He crossed to the breakfast tray on the table at the window. The street below was grey and empty. In the gutters, and close to the buildings where no one walked, slush still lay. Further on, one of the sluggish old buses had stopped with clouds of steam pouring from its worn carcass. In this mood, the steel gallows outline of the new government building down the street looked to him like something on the way down rather than on the way up.

He rejected the pineapple juice from Cuba, the butter from Poland, the boiled eggs tucked for warmth into a nest of knitted wool. He lit a cigarette and stirred sugar into his ersatz coffee. It was a situation for a strong, picturesque man, someone big and uniformed like Tito, buttressed by age and past glories. Who was Walter Eisler? Whom did he represent? He was the dark horse, the compromise candidate, who had won. The people hardly knew him. He hardly knew himself. He was weak and the trial had come when his energy was split between the conflicts of his private and his public life. He was ludicrously untrained and ill-equipped for the campaign. He was marching on Moscow, in winter, dressed in shorts and sandals.

Chapter Twenty

Woolcott was tinkering with a ballpoint pen.

'I thought you'd defected,' he said gruffly, screwing the ink cylinder back into the barrel.

'I got back very late,' Derby said. 'I took in a Schiller play at the Bertolt Brecht theatre while I was over there.' He hated himself for being so shamefaced about it.

'Which one?'

'*Marie Stuart*.'

Woolcott looked up. 'And had dinner at the *Gannymed*, I suppose?'

Derby gave a surprised smile. He was constantly being surprised by the odd little things that Woolcott knew about practically everything. He supposed that was why Woolcott was in charge. 'It was handy,' he said.

'It also serves the best food in East Berlin.'

'It was very good. Eisler used to go there regularly.' He felt it sounded like an attempt at an excuse.

'I waited here till eleven.' Woolcott's voice was reproachful.

'I caught the last S-bahn coming West.'

'Along with the separated lovers,' Woolcott said reflectively, as if visualising the tearful scenes as the People's Police came between East and West at the checkpoint. His eyes switched to Derby with a disconcerting clockwork motion that should have been accompanied by a click. 'Talking about lovers, how was young Mrs Sloane?'

Derby remembered without pleasure his last view of Margaret as she stood in the wide and windy main street of Potsdam watching the tramcar carry him back to the railway station. 'She hasn't changed,' he said. 'She isn't easy to impress. I told her where to contact me but . . .' he shook his head '. . . I'm pretty certain she won't come. Not just to talk to us. It was too vague.'

Woolcott had picked up the faulty ball point pen again and was making wide circles with it on a sheet of paper. Still the ink did not flow. 'Someone's making a fortune out of these,' he grumbled. 'All over the world people like us are wasting time trying to get these bloody things to write.' He dropped the pen into the waste bucket and sat looking over Derby's left shoulder for a few moments. 'It doesn't matter,' he said at last.

Derby looked at the pen lying in the bucket among the sheets of crumpled paper. 'I don't suppose so,' he said.

Woolcott did something with his tongue inside his mouth. 'Not the pen,' he said. 'I meant, it doesn't matter whether Mrs Sloane comes to see us or not.' He looked sideways into the bucket as if wondering if he should retrieve the pen and give it another chance. 'It would be better if she did, mind you, but it doesn't really matter.' He interlaced his long pink fingers and made the joints crack.

Resentment began to form in Derby but he did not speak.

'I suppose they did have someone following you?' Woolcott asked as if reproaching himself for not having inquired sooner.

'Oh, sure.'

'I hope they got a good look at you.'

Something almost as strong as hatred splashed about in Derby's liquid grey eyes. 'So, primarily, it wasn't to get her to talk to us?' He let his resentment show. 'All you wanted was for her to be seen with me. Why?'

'By now they'll know you work for us.'

'That's another thing,' Derby said angrily. 'That isn't going to make life any easier for me.'

Woolcott cracked his fingers again. 'It certainly means you can't go East for us again, but what the hell? This is your side of the Wall, Ramsden.' Derby knew the change in Woolcott's manner meant that he was trying to sound hearty. 'We just make sure you stay this side. It was worth letting them blow you.'

Derby tried sarcasm. 'Well, that's great.'

'Oh, don't look so huffed, Ramsden. It may be the most important thing you've ever done.'

Derby thought of various risks he had taken round the world. 'That makes me feel real important,' he said. *Real Special*, he thought, like something turned out by the woodcarvers of Oberammergau.

'Oh, don't be so bloody petty,' Woolcott said, with flaring, theatrical viciousness. 'What you feel doesn't matter. What I feel doesn't matter. The rockets are hot on the launch pads because of this guy Eisler and for all we know the world is on the edge of its last great darkness.'

Derby was shocked at the look in Woolcott's eyes. He was reminded of a hymn singer he had once seen at a gospel meeting. But even as he stared, Woolcott seemed to shrink. He turned away and when he spoke again his voice was almost apologetic.

'Since we started flying more troops in, the Russians down at the Air Safety Centre have been going crazy trying to think up reasons for blocking the air corridors. Things are getting really serious. It's like the Air Lift all over again. American, British and French tourists have been advised to give Berlin the go-by. All we need is for them to revive the Allied Komandatura and it'll be like old times.'

'I rather like the atmosphere,' Derby said, hoping that

the admission would annoy Woolcott. 'It's been bloody dull since I came here.'

'It's our job to keep it dull,' Woolcott said. 'And that's why you went East. If the Russians want to discredit Eisler and stick a talking doll in his chair, they've now got evidence of a direct link between him and us.'

Derby's mouth twisted contemptuously. 'But that's thin. Really thin.'

'Guys get shot over there every day on thinner stuff than that,' Woolcott said crisply. 'Friend Eisler would have a helluva time persuading a People's Court that an American agent was sleeping with him just for kicks.'

'If they think Mrs Sloane works for us she'll get the bullet as well.' It was difficult to know – perhaps difficult even for Derby himself to know – whether he was protesting or merely giving an opinion.

'No, she'd probably get off with a ten-year stretch. Anyway . . .' Woolcott put on his cataleptic expression again, rose slowly from his seat and started groping his way back to the window. 'We've thrown them a line.'

Chapter Twenty-One

Eisler spent the morning gathering figures that he felt would be useful when the talks with Kozhnev and the other Warsaw Pact leaders started at noon. These men, he knew, would be uninterested in the economic and humanitarian basis of his programme. They would come with closed minds. What they wanted was submission. They would want to unnerve him to the point where he would abandon the reforms completely or dilute them to the point of uselessness. Nevertheless, he intended to give them factual arguments.

Dmrycha of Bulgaria started the attack by citing the Greiffenberg arms raid as evidence that under Eisler's lax grip law and order were already breaking up in the DDR.

'It would never have happened,' Eisler said bitterly, 'but for the aggressive display to which our people are being treated. Force breeds force.'

'So does recklessness.' Kozhnev's eyes in daylight were puffier than ever. Was there something wrong with him? 'When Walter Ulbricht died he bequeathed to the SED a country at peace, not only with its neighbours, but with itself. By giving you, and men like you, their head within the existing Socialist philosophy he accomplished an economic miracle. In his term of power he created a country true to the people and to the principles of Social-ism. His successor was a man who walked the same wise path. Unfortunately, death cut his reign tragically short. In turn, you, a young man in politics, were given the chance of a wonderful future. What have you done with your inheritance?'

Kozhnev was looking at Eisler with what seemed to be genuine inquiry. In his face there was no sign of scorn or anger.

'In the few short months since your election you have endangered a great deal of what was left to you; the trust of your Warsaw Pact allies; the peace of mind of your people; the progress towards true sovereignty of your country; even your own personal future. Why?'

Again Kozhnev stopped and smiled in a disappointed way.

'I think because you are a good but inexperienced man. You have not yet resigned yourself to the imperfections of Socialism. You still seek perfection. Comrade . . .' his voice sharpened a little '. . . I can tell you that you will not find perfection on this earth. By the inevitable processes of evolution, by the gradual adaptations that are the material of human progress, I believe the Socialist communities of the world will move slowly in the direction that you are so prematurely signposting. But only a very small part of the journey will be accomplished in our lifetime.'

He lit a cigarette in the awkward way of a man who smokes infrequently. 'Comrades, in the privacy of this meeting, I confess to you that I am not one of those who believes in the decay of Capitalism and the triumph of world Socialism as propounded by Marx and Lenin. When I look at the great Capitalist societies, I do not see mouldering dinosaurs trapped in a prehistoric valley. I see vital organisms in the process of change. I see Capitalism adapting for survival. The dinosaur is growing wings to escape from its doomed valley. I see Capitalism taking to itself much of the Socialist philosophy, diluting and moulding it to its own needs. This is happening even in the United States of America, the headquarters of world

Capitalism. It has gone much further in Britain, France, West Germany, Italy, Japan, Canada . . . I could go on, but I have said enough to let you see that I do not subscribe to the theory that Capitalism or Communism must wither and die. I see these two systems moving towards a common centre. Perhaps it will take a hundred years. What is that? A blink in the eye of history.' He crushed out his cigarette. 'That for me is the time-scale of change. Unfortunately, Comrade Eisler wants to reform our society in a blink of the eye of man. No one doubts the sincerity of his intentions. But they are not reasonable. They are not safe. I hope we can convince him of this.'

Kozhnev's sympathy was soon lost in the acrimony that came with the harsh details of their fear and resentment.

Would Eisler guarantee that his foreign policy would harmonise on all important issues with that of his Communist allies? Could he be relied upon to have no separate economic or political ties with West Germany? Could he guarantee that an uncensored Press would not seek to curry favour with unhealthy elements by becoming critical of the Soviet Union? Was it true that one of his undisclosed ambitions was to opt out of the Warsaw Pact and seek to lead another, Westward-looking, Socialist bloc composed of Yugoslavia, Rumania and Czechoslovakia? Did he deny that he planned to purge from the Government, the Army and the diplomatic service some two thousand Old Guard supporters of the Ulbricht brand of progress, friends of the Soviet Union? Did a list of names exist? Endless extracts were read to him from Soviet publications. *Literaturnaya Gazete:* 'These wilful distortions of the Marxist-Leninist principles constitute a seditious attack on the Soviet system of fraternal and benevolent Government.' *Red Star*: 'The future defence of Eastern Europe is being endangered by the growth of hostile doctrines in East Germany.' How could he even consider, as they knew he was considering, sending a delegation to Washington in search of financial aid?

'Perhaps,' leered Prachl of Poland, 'because Comrade Eisler is already in receipt of considerable American aid and enjoys it so much that he craves for more.'

Coffee, beer and sandwiches were carried in at lunchtime so that the insults and demands could go on without halt. Another five hours passed before Kozhnev proposed that they adjourn for an hour. Outside, they were surrounded by reporters. Eisler stood white-faced and silent as Kozhnev smiled and brought out the phrases that he had practised all over Eastern Europe. Yes, perhaps the fraternal leaders might be showing some understandable concern at the proposals outlined in *Our Socialist Future*, but that was one purpose of the Pact, to create an atmosphere in which differences of opinion could be freely discussed. So far, they had reached full identity of views on all questions discussed.

Eisler left them to eat together and had a meal sent to his own office.

When they met again, the four of them settled silently, looking at him across the table like interrogators who have at last found the formula for cracking the prisoner.

'Would it not be best,' Kozhnev asked lightly, 'for you to stand down?' He made it sound like a trifle.

A grim smile broke on Eisler's tired face. 'Best for whom?' He felt calm and inexhaustibly stubborn.

'For everyone.'

'I don't think so.'

'Since you refuse to give us the assurances that we need, what else is there, other than military action?'

Eisler ignored the threat. 'The assurances you seek would mean the abandonment of the programme to which the Central Committee is committed. I have no mandate to abandon that programme.' It was an argument that he had given them six or seven times already and was prepared to give another dozen times if need be.

'It is the programme to which *you* are committed,' Kozhnev said. 'Without you, no such programme would ever have been presented to the Praesidium or to the Central Committee. Under different leadership I have no doubt the Central Committee would be prepared to amend its programme.'

'My resignation wouldn't help you much,' Eisler said wearily. 'The Praesidium is one hundred per cent in favour of the reforms to which you object. You wouldn't have anyone for my seat.'

Kozhnev smiled. 'Perhaps not quite one hundred per cent.'

'The minutes of our last meeting . . .'

'I am not interested in the records,' Kozhnev interrupted. 'There is a man whose sense of duty is stronger than any desire for cheap public popularity. He would be prepared to serve in your place.'

Eisler allowed none of the surprise that he felt to appear on his face. He tried to recall the speech that Zetkin had made to the Praesidium only two nights earlier, seeking to identify the opening through which he had now wriggled. Zetkin had seemed to commit himself completely, leaving no room for manoeuvre. Not that committal meant much in a power struggle. No doubt Zetkin would plead the good of the country and the interests of the party.

Eisler's shoulders ached so much that it was painful not to slouch across the table. 'Are you telling me that a member of the Praesidium is ready to betray a pledge freely given no more than forty-eight hours ago?'

'I am telling you,' Kozhnev said, 'that if you have the wisdom to stand down we have a man to take your place, a man with sufficient loyalty to the party and to the democratic struggle to shoulder the burden of your errors and to seek to redeem them.'

The distorted use of language infuriated Eisler. 'Who is this man?' he asked loudly. 'Why isn't he here?'

Kozhnev looked at the others. 'He could be here in a very few minutes. I will see to it. Then you can discuss the possibilities together.'

He lifted a telephone and spoke to one of the Russian officials who waited in an outer room. He looked inquiringly at Eisler. 'Would your private office be best?'

Twenty minutes later Eisler left the conference room and went upstairs to his own office on the third floor. Almost before he stepped into the room he knew who was there. The air was brown and greasy with the smoke of cheap pipe tobacco. The man standing in the shadows by the window was Albert Behrens, the only member of the Praesidium who had not been there to vote at the last meeting.

The old man came forward into the light cast by the lamp on Eisler's desk. He stood for a moment in silence, the pipe jutting from his pale face, his hands hanging stiffly from wrinkled sleeves.

His voice when it came was awkward. 'They didn't tell you, Walter?'

Eisler had turned away, his aching shoulders bowed as if under an enormous weight. 'No. They must have wanted to surprise me,' he said.

'Walter, try to understand. I couldn't refuse. They need me . . . the Party needs me. I am the only man acceptable to both reformers and traditionalists. I don't want it for myself. I'm an old man. I have no ambitions left. It would only be for a year or so.'

And then, thought Eisler, the carefully planned handover to Zetkin. Here was the explanation of Zetkin's speech. They had known that he would never stand down for Zetkin. But for Albert Behrens, they believed he might.

When he was able to look directly at the old man his voice was an accusing whisper. 'Now I know who you say all those prayers to, Albert. It's to the Devil.'

Behrens stood where he was.

'Not very long ago, Walter, you asked me if I thought there was a God. If there is, He will not ask me, when the time comes, if I lived Walter Eisler's life. He will ask if I lived Albert Behrens' life and listened to Albert Behrens' conscience.'

'And will He be happy with you when you say you have lived Karl Zetkin's life – or tried to live it – for a year?'

'I have given more than fifty years of my life to the Party. I cannot withhold what little time is left to me.'

Quite slowly, Eisler crossed the room. He put his hand on a crumpled sleeve and led the old man gently to the door.

'You'll find Kozhnev two floors down,' he said. 'Tell him the answer is still no. And tell him to leave old men in peace.'

Chapter Twenty-Two

Eisler locked the door after Albert Behrens and although someone knocked on it at intervals he remained slumped on his desk, his brow resting on his folded arms. The telephone rang two or three times, but he ignored it. He did not want to talk, even to Margaret.

All day he had been troubled by a terrible sense of injustice. Now, the treachery of Albert Behrens had drained him of the last drops of faith and resolution. There was no end to the Party's power to manipulate or suborn. All over the world, men were lying, dying and betraying for it; not out of wickedness, but from a burning sense of mission. The Party blinded certain men with the radiance of its vision. Eisler knew all this. He had himself used the terrible allure of the Party's ideas to extract from men sacrifices that would not otherwise have been forthcoming.

When the Party said dance, men danced. When the Party said die, men died with their hearts singing. Only the Roman Catholic Church could rival the Party for martyrs, and it had been in existence almost two thousand years longer. Already the Party had its own shrines. One day soon it would have its own international hagiolatry under the blessed trinity of Marx, Engels and Lenin; a calendar of saints headed by Guevara, Philby and Pontecorvo. Knowing all this, Eisler was still stunned at what Albert Behrens had done. Once, this man had fathered him. When his own father had been ill for months after his first heart attack, Albert Behrens had tutored Eisler in the evenings after school. On Sundays, Albert had taken him on the pleasure boats that sailed the Berlin lakes. Now, as he lay across his desk, Eisler longed to think of some awful pressure that the Party might have exerted to corrupt Albert Behrens. A sob shook through him. The only pressure was the monstrous evil of the Party's most cherished idea; that the good of the Party comes before the good of any man; before the good of ten thousand or ten million men. All at once, Eisler was immensely glad that his own father was dead and safe from the Party. What demands might the Party have been making now of his father if he had been alive? Whose side would his father have been on?

He raised his head from the desk, his mind yearning for reassurance. As he sat staring blindly across the room there came to him the notion that if he could not renew his strength from the things of this world, then perhaps he could draw on the energy – *grace* was the religious word for it – of the other world that was supposed to exist; the world to which his father had gone.

He lifted the telephone and ordered a car to meet him at the side entrance. Then he rang an aide and told him to pass on word that so far as he was concerned the talking was over for that day. He would be available to resume next morning.

In the side street, Comrade Zander held open the door of the Trabant until Eisler was seated. Then he climbed in beside the driver, who had turned to get his instructions from Eisler. Comrade Zander did not hear what was said. Where would it be to-night, he wondered. The flat? The villa in the official compound? The arms of Mrs Sloane in the house near Potsdam? Comrade Zander realised that if the choice was his the car would turn left at the foot of the badly lit street and head fast for Mrs Sloane. A picture of Margaret's strongly etched face came to him in the warm darkness and he realised for the first time that it was the same type of face as Gerda Kopf's.

These were the sharp-nosed, bright-eyed faces, he thought, of women who dug their way through life, shovelling it aside in confident spade loads. It was not just chance that had turned Fräulein Kopf to tunnelling. She had been created for it. The thought filled Comrade Zander with happy amusement. He felt so warm and drowsy that he did not even notice which way the car turned at the foot of the empty street.

Eisler noticed. He remembered the route from more than twenty years ago. He closed his eyes and flooded his mind with a picture of the funeral procession driving slowly in badly kept pre-war cars through streets lined with the stumps and splinters of bomb ruins. The rebuilding of Berlin had hardly started then, especially in the Communist sector. That had been long before the Wall and there had been more sign in those days that it was a city nominally under four-power rule. Russian, British, American and French troops had intermingled throughout the four sectors. The fiction was still maintained, of course, with East and West still sending token patrols into the opposing zones. Some of the old streets had vanished in the Slav-inspired reconstruction of this city of the Teutons. His father, who had managed to combine his Communist faith with a perverse love of the great buildings of Imperial Germany, would hardly recognise Berlin if he could see it now.

Gone the hotels of Unter den Linden and the cafes where writers and artists met. Gone the great Royal Schloss of the Hohenzollerns to make room for a square dedicated to Marx and Engels. What would his father have made of the television tower in Alexanderplatz with its gardens and restaurants rotating 1,200 feet up in the sky, built while the people still lacked fresh fruit and many other commodities that were commonplace across the Wall?

A wandering searchlight beam from the Wall flashed across the car. How many would die out there to-night?

They were driving westwards. Soon the street lights thinned and stopped. The frosted roof of an occasional house glinted coldly in the moonlight. A few minutes later the car slowed and turned into a narrow, unpaved lane. It bumped along for about half a mile and then stopped. On one side of the lane fields stretched whitely to where the lights of a new suburban housing estate formed a speckle of brightness and warmth. On the other side of the lane there was a cemetery, bounded by a wall from which the coping and upper courses of random stone were crumbling.

Eisler got out of the car and, ignoring Comrade Zander's surprised gaze, pushed open the broken iron gates. He could see quite well and he found his father's grave without difficulty. He stood looking at it, shivering a little, wondering why he was there.

He had come with some vague idea of praying. Now, all he could do was stand on the frozen path gazing at the lumpy, weed-covered earth and the moss-grown stone that bore his father's name, thinking about his father in a confused and wandered way. His father had never been anything higher in the Party than secretary of an unimportant branch in an industrial suburb of Berlin. He had never been in a Nazi prison nor in Moscow in the hotel near Gorky Street that the Comintern kept for exiled German Communists. His father had fought only once in the streets and he had suffered a heart attack for it. What had he been fighting for? To see one half of the world living in fear of the other? To have Berlin divided by a Wall? To have the workers shot by their own Communist guards? Had he fought to replace the heel of

Hitler with the heel of Moscow? Eisler was certain that his father had been fighting the same fight that he was fighting now, for a benevolent Socialism under which there would be enough for all but where, also, effort would be rewarded; where sound economic principles would not be smothered under dogma; where men could write and speak as they pleased; where exploiters of the people would vanish instead of simply wearing new labels.

A cold wind was blowing across the rows of moonlit graves and above him the supple branches of birch trees flicked restlessly at the sky. He straightened uneasily, like a sleeper disturbed, as there came on the wind the sound of a shot, then three or four more shots. He shuddered. Even here it was impossible to escape reminders of the forces that he had unloosed. The border with West Berlin was less than a mile away across the fields at Klein-Machnow. He listened, but no more shots came. What he heard was the sound of footsteps behind him and then he felt a hand touch his arm.

'Please,' Comrade Zander said softly. 'The car may attract attention at this hour. The patrols are very active now all along the border area.'

Eisler began to tremble again. His face felt cold and strangely solid. What had brought him here? A sense of shame confused him further as he realised that it must be at least ten or twelve years since he had last visited his father's grave. Some of the weeds were almost a foot high. Was such neglect forgivable?

As he saw the concern in Comrade Zander's normally wary eyes he forced himself to think of everyday things; letters that had to be answered, visits that had to be made to new building sites or factories with expansion pro-grammes.

He was appalled at his own weakness and at his almost total unfittedness for the dangerous road he had taken.

After a few weeks of strain he was on the verge of a nervous collapse. In similar circumstances a Tito or a Ceausescu would have grown.

'I hadn't realised how cold it was,' he said in an attempt to explain his trembling. He looked about uncertainly, wondering which of the many paths he had come by.

'It will be warm in the car,' Comrade Zander said as he took Eisler's arm again and led him back between the creaking trees in the vague white light from the frosty sky.

Chapter Twenty-Three

Next morning, Kozhnev said: 'Let us talk to-day about the Wall and your desire to take it down.'

He sounded, Eisler thought, like a psychiatrist launching a new stage in the treatment of a patient suffering from some obscure iconoclastic urge. He tried to think of parts the other three might play; possibly sinister foreign attendants ready to rush him back to the padded cell if he became violent. Vaguely he was aware of Kozhnev's voice.

'Have you had any support for this move? I mean, in the world beyond the Praesidium and Central Committee of the S E D?'

More than ever he was managing to make it sound like an aberration.

Eisler closed his eyes and tried to remember how many lights there were in the chandelier above the table; the prisoner keeping his sanity by ticking off the days on a home-made calendar.

Half way through the morning there was a long silence which ended with Kozhnev flapping noisily through his notes and going into a detailed review of the Wall's history. In the middle of it, Eisler realised that Kozhnev was desperate to keep the talk going. The threats had failed along with the pleas. The hope that he would bow out for Albert Behrens had been snuffed. Kozhnev was like a conjurer faced either with keeping the patter going or confessing that there is no rabbit in the hat.

Kozhnev was saying: '. . . a massive fortification which also involves trenches, trip wires, underwater barricades and the death-strip area of almost two thousand square kilometres.'

Eisler's head nodded. He had been awake for most of the night. Kozhnev was saying: 'Remember, in eleven years before the Wall the D D R lost a sixth of its population, including 40,000 members of the People's Army.'

An absurd picture came to Eisler of a country totally abandoned except for a Government that passed the same law over and over again, demanding that everyone come back.

He was smiling faintly as he said: 'This is the first time I have heard anyone of your stature admit that the Wall was built to stop people leaving. Ulbricht and Khruschev called it a *Peace Protection Dam*, built to keep out the Western imperialists.'

He felt almost sorry now for Kozhnev, sitting there holding his empty, rabbitless hat.

'I think we can leave Ulbricht and Khruschev out of this,' Kozhnev said lamely.

*

Again Eisler excused himself from eating with them. He went to his office and spent the two-hour break telephoning or seeing other members of the Government and in reading the reports stacked on his desk in neatly-typed bundles.

During the night another three people had been shot dead on the Wall. Five had been wounded.

The familiarity of these incidents had gradually dulled their horror and the real shock to Eisler was a report that after more than twenty-five years of co-operation, the Russians had withdrawn from the joint air safety centre in the American sector of West Berlin. This act was a

eprisal for the Allied use of the Berlin air corridors to fly
n troops. Down the years, the sanctity of the air corridors
had been preserved. Now, not only had the Russians dis-
continued co-operation, they were planning to harass all
Western flights in and out of Berlin by jamming radio and
radar signals. Arguments had gone on all of the previous
day. The air corridors, according to the Russians, had
been established over the Soviet Occupied Zone of
Germany as necessary supply routes for the peaceful
Allied administration of West Berlin. Their use as pipe-
lines for the pumping in of thousands of fighting troops
was a violation of their purpose, a provocation to the
Soviet Union and to the D D R and an irresponsible threat
to world peace. The Allies had already replied with notes
of protest and pointed out that if flight plans were no
longer to be interchanged then they would be forced to
supply flights to West Berlin with fighter escorts.

And the inevitable and potentially deadly retaliation
to that, Eisler thought, as he read the grim digests, will be
Russian fighters 'buzzing' Allied air traffic.

He riffled through a few more pages but all he could
find was menace.

Marshal Ivan Yakubovsky, Commander-in-Chief of
the Warsaw Pact forces, had arrived in Berlin from
Bucharest to confer with General Servia, the officer
commanding the Russian manoeuvres. The threat was
clear to Eisler; from being a Soviet invasion it could be
turned into a concerted assault on the D D R by practically
the whole of Communist Europe.

As he read on, the telephone rang. It was one of
his secretaries to tell him that Karl Zetkin was making
an unannounced appearance on television. He switched
on.

'I was a party,' Zetkin was saying, 'to the Praesidium's
decision to implement the programme of reform set out

in a document that has become known as *Our Socialist Future*. This document has been accepted by the Central Committee of the SED and is therefore now official policy. Although it has not yet been published you all know its contents. They have put Europe in ferment. From the beginning, this programme seemed to me to be far too bold. But how could I deny its ideals?

'I have given them my vote in the Praesidium and I declare my support for them now before the whole nation. However, I now also declare my belief that it is an adventurous, vain and romantic illusion for any man . . .' (That's me, Eisler thought) '. . . to imagine that such momentous changes can be applied simultaneously or even gradually in the present climate of resentment and fear that this programme has inspired among our Socialist neighbours. I would further declare that it is a low aspiration on the part of any man to proceed with this programme in the face of such forces as are at present aligned against it. Already the foolhardy haste has given rise to a lamentable situation which can only encourage anti-Socialist forces everywhere and deflect the course of proletarian internationalism. Because of this, I call for a six-month postponement of this programme. Such a voluntary gesture on our part would, I believe, lead to a beginning of normalisation.'

Eisler switched off. He should have been angry but all he felt was a vague surprise that Zetkin should have made such a mistimed declaration of his true intent. No one in the Party would be deluded by the talk of a postponement. Zetkin clearly reckoned that in six months such a pressure could be mounted that Eisler would have to resign or be promoted to obscurity.

It was a rash, unsanctioned speech that exposed Zetkin's position but left everyone else's unaffected. It would be remembered against him both for its content and for the fact that he had delivered it several days too late. It might even be Zetkin's epitaph.

*

As they gathered again after lunch the sound of cheering came into the long frescoed room.

Eisler walked to the window. The sleet that had been falling since morning had stopped, leaving the patch of afternoon sky above the square a more monotonous grey than ever. The city seemed drained of colour, like the faces of the people gathered below. Since Kozhnev's arrival Marx-Engels-Platz had been filled with people. They stood all day outside Central Committee HQ in anxious silence, swathed in heavy coats and boots. Whenever an official car drew up the crowd moved stiffly forward in eerie silence. Even when the recognisable leaders arrived or departed they were treated to the same uncanny quiet and the gaze of expressionless eyes. Eisler had noticed that the crowd was made up mainly of the middle-aged or the old, the generations which had known a day when there were no Russians in Central Europe.

These were the people who had pushed barrows and handcarts through the ruins of Berlin in 1945, a Berlin smashed into uncountable fragments, but still united, even if only in misery. They had been raped and robbed by the Russians, bought by the British and Americans for a few cigarettes, dragooned by their own countrymen who had come back triumphantly to puppet-power from the long exile in Moscow, and they had gathered into this same mute mass in August, 1961, to watch the Wall going up, cementing them in, sealing hope out. Superficially, they seemed ordinary enough people, but they always reminded Eisler of the public buildings that the regime had taken so much care in reconstructing. The frontages looked the same, but from most of them the old heart and purpose had gone.

Three armoured cars were moving slowly along the south side of the square. The crowd, which had shunned the troops taking part in the manoeuvres, were, for some reason that Eisler could not understand, greeting these soldiers like liberators.

Several more bursts of cheering rattled back from the new buildings lining Marx-Engels-Platz before Eisler realised that these were not Russian vehicles. One was American, one British, one French. He could see quite clearly now the foreign markings and the uniforms of the crews. The excited people had closed in around the cars and reduced their progress to a crawl. Even from the window, Eisler could see the surprised grins on the faces of the Allied soldiers and sense the warmth in the hands that the people held up to them.

As he listened to the hubbub and watched the waving scarves and handkerchiefs, a strange exultation began to rise in Eisler's heart, but even as it started he was ashamed and suspicious of it. It was incredible that he should be thinking of these soldiers almost as friends. These were the blood-stained warmongers, imperialist aggressors and hyena beasts of a hundred thousand Communist speeches delivered annually from Albania to Peking. He had himself denounced the Governments behind these men in the old familiar phrases. What had happened to his reasoning?

Kozhnev and the others were gazing into the square in puzzlement. So dense now was the crowd that the three armoured cars had stopped. No traffic was moving in the square or in the streets that led from it.

Five or six Vopos pushed their way through the crowd. They gestured and shouted to the occupants of the armoured cars. The young officers in charge of the expedition looked embarrassed and pointed helplessly to the solid barricade of cheering people. The Vopos paused and looked at each other undecidedly. Eisler knew what was going to happen. He wanted to throw open the window and shout an order. Instead, he watched the Vopos draw their batons. For a moment the cheering stopped as the people realised what was happening. The exuberant sounds changed to screams as the batons came down. Suddenly there was an angry roar. The mass of people tightened, then undulated, and within seconds the Vopos were engulfed and lost in a huge wave of shouting men and women.

'What is happening? Who are these soldiers?' It was the anxious voice of Prachl, from Poland.

'It is a patrol from West Berlin,' Eisler said. In his head, he had rejected these men from the other side of the Wall but the situation was such a defeat for the baffled men beside him that he could hardly keep the satisfaction from his voice.

'Then where is your military? Why is there no resistance?'

'Resistance?' Eisler looked at Prachl with contempt. He was an excited barrel of a man in a badly made suit and the talks had shown him to be the kind of crude Communist who believes in standing on anything that offends him. 'You are quite safe, Comrade,' Eisler said. 'We have not been invaded. These soldiers are entitled to be here.'

Dmrycha stretched forward inquiringly. 'In armoured cars?'

'Would you expect them to patrol in taxis? The Russians still send armoured cars into the British, American and French sectors.'

He turned to get Kozhnev's agreement. What he saw was the Russian's face tense with anger, the eyes bruised

151

with emotion above two grey sacks of puffed-out skin.

'Get them out of there,' Kozhnev said violently. Under the hopeless strain of trying to keep his rage hidden, his chin seemed to break away from his face at the lower corners of his mouth, suggesting the mechanical trap of a ventriloquist's doll.

'On what grounds? Berlin is still under four-power rule.'

'They are not entitled to stage a parade in our sector or bring the traffic to a halt.'

'They are not parading.'

Eisler was only beginning to realise the enormity of the affront to Kozhnev. Here was the universal Communist father being treated to the sound and sight of his East German children openly declaring their preference for the unprincipled debauchees of Paris, London and Washington.

'Our people are friendly to everyone,' Eisler said without much hope of being believed. 'All that noise means very little.'

The remark only inflamed Kozhnev. 'It is an insane Imperialist provocation.' His voice was almost a shout. He pointed to a telephone but kept looking at Eisler. 'If your police cannot break up that crowd then the Red Army will.'

'That would be the worst possible thing you could do.' Eisler lifted the telephone. 'You have created enough trouble without involving yourself in a trifling civil incident.'

'Trifling! These people are insulting the Soviet Union and its Warsaw Pact Allies.'

Dmrycha moved uneasily towards Kozhnev. 'It could be dangerous,' he said diffidently. 'If there should be an incident between the Red Army and the men in those armoured cars . . .' He shrugged. 'Perhaps Comrade

Eisler is right. It is perhaps a matter for the People's Police.'

Police reinforcements had arrived in the square and were being greeted with shouts of 'Gestapo! Gestapo!'

Kozhnev turned his back to the window. In the dejected line of the broad shoulders Eisler recognised a fellow victim. Here was another man being tortured by doubts about the course he had taken.

Chapter Twenty-Four

There are three night bars in East Berlin. One – the *Opernbar* – is in the basement of the Opera House. Tables there are awarded like passes to the West. There is no membership, but entry is almost entirely by introduction. At the door, the People's State ends. No real worker has ever been inside, except to work. Here, high officials and industrialists entertain important visitors to smoked salmon, genuine Moselle and Western dance music. From time to time a few surviving owners of private businesses come, a little forlornly, to pretend that nothing has really changed.

And here, a few hours after Kozhnev had declared the talks abandoned, Eisler came with Margaret. As the official aircraft flew out of Schonfeld for Moscow, Warsaw, Sofia and Budapest, Eisler and Margaret danced and clapped hands as a blonde in a white dress sang *Arrivederci, Hans*.

As the music ended, Margaret said: 'You still haven't told me if this is a celebration or an act of defiance.'

In the last week she had become thinner and more fragile but in a way that made him think not of illness or frailty, but of beauty. She was wearing a short blue dress that every woman in the room must have known had come from outside the DDR and her hair was too neat to have been set any earlier than that afternoon. She at least, Eisler thought, had decided it was a celebration. The hair style seemed to accentuate the grey resignation of her eyes. As he looked down at her he was filled with an enormous hope that, somehow, they would have a future together.

'Let's just call it an intermezzo,' he said. 'It seems like years since I last relaxed and enjoyed myself.'

She gave him a sympathetic smile. 'I'd say you're about as relaxed now as a high tension spring.'

In the crisis weeks his face had become known and as they went back to their table people saluted shyly as he passed.

'Everyone here seems to approve of you, anyway,' Margaret said. 'When that dance finished they were applauding for you as much as for the band.'

'Maybe they've heard that Kozhnev has gone home.' His expression was sardonic.

'And they are taking it as a victory for you.' She leaned across the table. 'It is a victory, Walter, isn't it?'

It was too soon, Eisler thought, to admit anything yet, but at the end there had been an expression in Kozhnev's eyes that could have been taken as a signal, if not of defeat, then of indefinite withdrawal.

He made some encouraging noises and then realised that she was nodding towards the next table. He turned and saw a man and woman in their fifties. She wore a tinselly cocktail dress and he was in a dark suit of hard VEB cloth. They looked like shopkeepers on a night out. The man's expression was apologetic but the woman was holding her glass and smiling. As Eisler turned she said: 'We know who you are and we would like to thank you.'

He made an embarrassed acknowledgement.

'The people know that what you want is right.' She was affected by the wine and the gaiety but even so she hesitated. 'We are Germans,' she said daringly, 'not Communists. We have a little prayer in our house. It has only two words. *Ein Berlin.*'

Ein Volk! Ein Reich! Ein Fuhrer! The Nazi slogans had

led to carnage. He wondered would *Ein Berlin* be so different?

'*Ein Berlin*,' the woman's husband repeated, nodding with timorous approval.

The woman gave him a fond look. 'My husband is Willy,' she said to Eisler. 'And I am Ruth.' She was fumbling in her purse with two fingers. As she found what she was looking for, she said: 'This is my talisman. If you would accept it, perhaps it would be lucky for all of us.'

She was holding out a West German One Mark piece. Eisler took it with an amused smile and thanked her. Everybody seemed to think he had changed camps.

Chapter Twenty-Five

Garkov's broken voice was sharp with bitterness.

'You've been tricked by a Jewish jackal.'

Kozhnev gestured impatiently. 'He's not a Jew. And I haven't been tricked.'

'And what about the healthy elements?' Garkov asked. 'Have we deserted them?'

'They have no leaders.'

'There is certainly Zetkin. Bahr is another possibility.'

'Zetkin?' Kozhnev looked depressed. 'He is ambitious but ineffectual. He is useless to us in this situation. As for Bahr, he has remained in shadow. He is devious.'

Garkov made his spitting noise. 'At least they are loyal. Not like that Zionist, Eisler.'

'Zetkin and Bahr command too little support in the Praesidium. They are too unsure of themselves. Zetkin has miscalculated badly. On top of his indecision, he made a mistaken speech on television. There's too much of what the English call the fop in him.'

'And Albert Behrens? Tell me his weaknesses.'

'Behrens would allow himself to be co-opted if Eisler resigned, but he will not fight him. He is old.'

'Wah! It is us who should be fighting him.' Garkov dropped his cigarette and ground it angrily into the polished wood floor.

'There will be no fighting.' Kozhnev rose from his desk and walked to the window. 'I have already ordered General Servia to terminate the manoeuvres. The last of our troops will have been withdrawn from the Wall by midnight.' He turned to face Garkov. 'That was a bluff that I will never repeat.'

Garkov's face twisted. 'You sound frightened, Comrade.'

'Yes, Ivan, I have been frightened.' A faint smile moved across Kozhnev's tired face. 'I have been afraid every hour of the day since our troops went on the Wall. One incident with the other side could have led to a situation from which neither of us could retreat.' He returned moodily to his desk. 'I do not see myself as the architect of world destruction.'

'There would be no destruction. They are too decadent to fight, these people.'

'You are wrong. In Berlin, in the faces of the people, I saw fear. But I also saw hatred. Hatred of our soldiers. And I sensed desperation. Even with twenty or thirty divisions of troops we could not quell these people as easily as we did in 1953. A vision has been presented to them. They are desperate for it to become a reality. What I felt in Berlin was the atmosphere of war. I am not ashamed to admit that I shrank from it. The German people would rise against us if we took Eisler from them.'

Garkov snorted. 'Rise against us with what? Sticks and stones?'

'The raid on our arms store at Greiffenberg was a sign of what we could expect. With China threatening Vladivostock and Khabarovsk the last thing we want is an East Germany peopled by partisans.'

'I've discussed all that with Malishniev,' Garkov said, shaking his bald head. 'East Germany is not partisan country. It is a featureless land. Tito has the only partisan terrain in the Communist bloc.'

'No matter. There are other reasons why we should not impose our will on Eisler by force. To do so would be to destroy our good relations with the West. For almost hree years I have devoted myself to reburnishing our world image. When I succeeded to this office our name was at its lowest since the blackest days of Stalin's Cold War. The glory gained for us by our space programme and our achievements in science had been frittered away by the clumsiness of the men who sat at this desk before me. To-day, the Soviet Union is respected in the world as it has not been since the days of our epic stand against Hitler's armies. I will not have that taken from us because of Eisler. I will not have Europe plunged into another Cold War. I will not have my work destroyed.'

'I will! I will! I will!' Garkov was staring as if astonished. 'For your pride,' he said, 'the Soviet Union is to be deprived of its greatest bulwark against Federal Germany. Is that what you are saying?'

'You know that's not what I am saying.'

'You are worried about the history books,' Garkov said, as if pronouncing a final shaming judgment. 'The history books of the West.'

Kozhnev leaned back wearily in his chair.

'We tried to frighten Eisler and we failed. Now we are going to leave him to his own Praesidium. Let him launch his unworkable programme. We must hope that when they begin to feel their grip on the country loosening they will find a way of deposing him.'

'And if they don't?'

Kozhnev closed his eyes and let his head fall limply backwards. 'I am tired, Ivan,' he said. 'For to-night we have talked enough.'

Book Two

Chapter Twenty-Six

Fräulein Kopf looked wan and Comrade Zander did not think it was simply because the flame-tinted desk lamp was out. To-day, her dark glasses suggested not so much hot sand and *Ambre Solaire* as the blindness of a Siberian white-out. Comrade Zander shivered a little as he watched her riffle through a few of her index cards. How could she keep up the pretence?

'You've got me baffled, Freddi,' she said, looking at him with a mixture of dejection and irritation. 'I don't seem able to place you at all. I was certain you would hit it off with Carla.'

Comrade Zander shuddered at the thought of Carla, but he did not speak. There was nothing to say about Carla that he had not already said about Eva, Lotte, Lena and one or two others.

All at once, as he looked across the narrow desk, he realised that it was someone like Gerda Kopf that he wanted. Like? Like? No. It was Gerda Kopf herself that he wanted. Or was it Margaret Sloane? He could hardly tell one from the other now. Not physically, of course, for the kinship of these two women lay far below the visible shell. He had known Gerda Kopf only for a month or two. Could you love a woman in so short a time? He had known Margaret for five or six months. To know one was to know the other. Five added to one made six. You could certainly love a woman – two women – in six months.

Fräulein Kopf was saying: 'Carla is a very nice, smart, intelligent girl who has a responsible job and takes an interest in most things.'

'There must be something wrong with her or she wouldn't have to come here.' Comrade Zander's voice was rebellious.

Fräulein Kopf looked at him sharply. 'Now don't start that again, Freddi. We've been through all that.'

'It's true. You know it's true. People don't come here because of a Loving Hand. There's no Loving Hand.'

She opened a drawer and shut it again with a bang. 'You come here, too, you know. Is there something wrong with you?'

'Yes,' he said. 'I'm a freak.'

Her angry expression softened. 'Don't say or even think that about yourself, Freddi. You're small and sensitive and possibly a little too introverted and your attitude to women is perhaps just a bit too much on the old-fashioned side. You seem to expect a girl out of a cameo brooch, but that doesn't make you a freak.'

'Doesn't it?' Comrade Zander chortled self-pityingly as he turned away from her to stare out at the wilderness of empty buildings and bombed sites where Vopos prowled and Border troops patrolled with dogs.

'No, it doesn't.' He was confused to hear her voice trembling. 'It means you have an ideal, maybe an unreachable ideal, but better that than . . . than . . .'

To his astonishment, something that he had several times suspected to be taking place behind Fräulein Kopf's sunglasses, quite clearly was happening now. A small, strangely beautiful tear was trickling down the side of her nose. She made no attempt to hide it.

'What's wrong?'

'You didn't know I was married, did you, Freddi?'

As he looked at her ringless fingers something choking rose in his throat, making it impossible for him to answer.

Oh, my God, he thought, if these poor dumb lips could

only speak. He had an enormous desire to take her hand and place it on his breast so that she would be aware of his thumping heart.

'I've spoken to him on the telephone while you've been here, but you wouldn't know.'

He remembered two or three occasions when her voice had been curt and strained as she spoke on the telephone but he had assumed it to be guilt; something to do with the tunnel. It was strange to think of it lying there beneath them. 'No,' he said. 'I didn't know.'

'I'm divorcing him. I'll have to shut this place down soon.' She looked round the featureless room as if she would miss it.

'Why?' He felt shaken.

'With the divorce coming up it would make me look ridiculous, running a marriage bureau.'

Was this the truth? What was she saying? It couldn't be the truth. They were either finished with the tunnel or they felt it was becoming too dangerous.

He was suddenly afraid for her. It *was* too dangerous. The Border troops. The Vopos. The SSD. Sooner or later things would begin to close in on her. Already there was a cut-off feeling about the small room, as if snow lay high in the corridors and wolves were gathering at the door. It was a terrible thought that Fräulein Kopf might soon disappear along the tunnel for the last time.

Comrade Zander had an immense wish to comfort her, to say something soothing that would end these tears which he could not understand, but which hurt him. His mouth opened hesitantly and then trembled shut. He realised with shame that the language of comfort was one that he had never learned. Was it too late now?

He said: 'Is there no hope?' They were talking about different things but only he knew that. For the first time, he began to suspect the meaning of the term heartbreak, and to know what parting meant. He thought of Eisler and Margaret.

Fräulein Kopf shook her head. 'We've lived apart for a long time. But it's still sad. Forgive me for crying. And thank you, Freddi, for not laughing.'

'Laughing?' He was shocked.

'Well, it's funny, when you think that I'm trying to get other people married.'

'No,' Comrade Zander said. 'It's tragic. Must you close this place?' He felt almost as he had felt when he had been told that his mother was dying.

'Yes, I'd have to have closed it, anyway. It's been costing me too much money. You know, Freddi . . .' she leaned across the desk like a prisoner who had decided to tell everything '. . . I haven't arranged a single marriage.'

Of course she hadn't, but he knew now that on this level, as well, she was suffering. He knew that, tunnel or not, she really did care for him and all the other misfit people in her index file. He felt the exaltation of a strange emotion which he took to be pity. 'You haven't been established long enough,' he said with desperate tenderness. 'That's all. People are sometimes engaged for years.' He tried to smile and remembered that he was supposed to be in the wine trade. 'After all, it takes a long time to produce a good blend.'

She looked at him gratefully. 'No. There's hardly anyone left now. There isn't another girl on the cards I could honestly introduce you to.' She smiled briefly. 'Maybe you'll be able to write a poem about all this some day. *The Ballad of Gerda Kopf*. Or maybe an elegy would be more appropriate.'

He heard himself saying: 'Gerda . . . I know about . . .' He pointed at the floor. 'About down there. I know about it, but you don't have to worry. I won't tell.'

Chapter Twenty-Seven

A fat grey pigeon peered in from the window sill as if considering Woolcott's head as a possible site for a nest. Woolcott was pale but resolute looking.

'It's the sort of situation we were created for.' He spoke as if he expected to be contradicted. 'When political means fail . . .' He made an irritable gesture as Derby tried to speak. His voice became more emphatic. 'The Russians have left me with no choice. We must deal with the Eisler problem ourselves.'

'But if they're happy to let him get on with it . . .' Derby was stopped by another wave of the hand.

'They cannot be happy, Ramsden. They are simply afraid of world opinion.'

'It amounts to the same thing.'

'Only in the short run. In the long run they will have to defy world opinion and crush him. By that time he might be so involved with Federal Germany and the West that we would have to side with him. If that ever happened . . .'

Woolcott stopped and puffed his cheeks out. 'This is what was in the President's mind when he said Eisler was a threat to world peace. Like me, he was worried *not* that Eisler might not get away with it, but that he *would* get away with it. The President will be a very worried man to-day.'

'I don't see what we can do.' Derby was staring fixedly at a painting which showed the faded and blackened head and shoulders of a man from some other age wearing a jabot, a red waistcoat and a fluffy, female hair-do. It had been left in a cupboard by the previous occupants but it was vaguely like Woolcott in fancy dress. 'The Russians tried to overthrow him. We tried to help them...'

'Yes. Our seeds appear to have fallen on stony ground.' Woolcott's voice was solemn. 'In any case, there's a much more certain way.'

Suddenly Derby's tongue felt too big for his mouth. 'What's that?' he asked awkwardly.

'We can remove Eisler ourselves.'

'You're talking now about . . .' Derby was astonished to find that he could not go on.

Woolcott seemed to be trying to look shy. 'Yes, Ramsden, I am talking about Eisler's death, and believe me, I do not like playing God.'

'You can't do that on your own . . .'

From the window sill the pigeon watched glassily.

'We were put here to act on our own, Ramsden.'

'I won't do it.' Derby's expression was ludicrously rebellious.

Woolcott looked at him in surprise and then began to laugh. 'Oddly enough, I hadn't thought of you.'

A sigh shuddered through Derby's out-of-condition body. 'Who else have you?'

'The world is full of people with strange pathological urges.'

'I've never had to work with them before,' Derby said, and then wondered eerily if he was talking to one now.

Woolcott's voice had gone placatory. 'No office like this can work without them, Ramsden. We have our special responsibilities.'

'Have you asked about this?'

'Asked?'

'Have you had the OK?'

Woolcott took the impertinent question on a walk to the window, but when he turned he was smiling.

'Let us say that when it happens no one will be too surprised.'

Derby began to look relieved. He hesitated. 'I still don't see what good it'll do.'

'*Our Socialist Future* is Eisler's child. No successor will push it with the same enthusiasm.'

'If it's as simple as that, why didn't the Russians murder him themselves?'

'Because the world would have branded them for it,' Woolcott said softly.

'But, Christ Almighty, the world will brand them for it, anyway, even if we do it.' As he stopped speaking, an unbelieving expression came on to Derby's reddened face.

Woolcott nodded, conveying both triumph and re-straint. 'That's right, Ramsden.' He sucked two or three clouds of smoke from his glass pipe. 'There are some situations in which you simply cannot win. In this situation the Russians are the all-time losers. I think it was that which really cut the most ice with them back home.'

Chapter Twenty-Eight

Only Woolcott knew that the bureau maintained another two small rooms above a row of dingy shops behind Bleibtreustrasse. In this outpost Woolcott made the arrangements for Eisler's death.

Rain splashed from the broken gutters and ran down the unwashed windows as he sat at a bare table opposite a thin, middle-aged man who still wore his wet coat, hat and gloves.

'A room has been reserved for you at the Hilton.' Woolcott's English had become Europeanised and he wore a black leather coat buttoned to the neck. 'Leave wherever you are staying now and check in there to-morrow afternoon. They welcome you there with a free champagne cocktail. Go to the downstairs bar at about eight o'clock to drink it before dinner. While you are there a man called Sneyder will speak to you. Next morning you will drive into East Berlin as a tourist. Sneyder will have given you an address in East Berlin where you will collect the rifle. At this same address you will be joined by a man to whom you will hand over your car. He will drive for you.'

The man on the other side of the table eased his soggy hat back a little. The hat was too tight and a red line showed where the rim had cut into his pale skin. He seemed to be bald. Woolcott had never seen him without his hat. He had employed him several times but all he really knew about him was that his name was Cavers and that he owned a small pottery in Liege which made ornamental wine flasks.

'Where do I get the car?' Cavers had smudged his forehead with the dye from his wet gloves. Woolcott wondered if he should mention it, but the moment passed.

'The car will be waiting for you in the street when you leave here. This is a duplicate set of keys.' He pushed them across the table, almost hesitantly, a look of slight concern on his face. 'Please make a point of filling the tank with petrol before you cross East. It is a new English Rover V8 and I don't want it abused more than can be helped.' Woolcott smiled apologetically. 'At times I run it myself. East German petrol is cheaper but even a little of it corrodes the cylinder heads. Besides . . . for your own safety . . . the extra octanes in West petrol will give you an advantage if it should come to high-speed driving.'

'I have never driven this English . . . Rover.' Cavers said the word as if it displeased him.

Woolcott became enthusiastic. 'Oh, you will like it. The transmission is automatic, the acceleration . . .' he lifted his hands towards the ceiling '. . . there is nothing like it east of the Brandenburg Gate. The road-holding is better even than . . .'

As he saw Cavers' look of disinterest his faint worry about the safety of the car returned. He had promised to take someone for a run in it at the week-end. 'You will remember to fill the tank this side? The doorman at the Hilton will . . .' He stopped again as he saw that Cavers wanted to speak.

'What make is the rifle?'

Woolcott looked about the bare table as if he had a few invisible notes there.

'I understand it will be an East German Army Schwarze with telescopic lense, minimum recoil, high muzzle-velocity, low trajectory . . .' He shrugged as if further technicalities were beyond him. If Cavers wasn't interested in the car, he wasn't interested in the gun. 'Will that be suitable?'

'There are others I prefer. The Schwarze is heavy. The ammunition clips are bulky. But, yes . . . it is a good firearm.'

Woolcott rose from the table. He seemed to notice for the first time that Cavers' coat was very wet. He said: 'The hotel you are in to-night is comfortable? They will dry your things?'

Cavers pulled the shapeless hat back down on his brow and smiled for the first time. 'You would not like me to catch cold, eh? It would ruin your plans?'

Woolcott looked uncomfortable. 'The driver you will collect in East Berlin knows where to take you. He will know when to take you. He will indicate the target.' He crossed briskly to the door and opened it.

Cavers hesitated. 'I sometimes like to know what they have done,' he said.

Something surprising happened to Woolcott's face. In the bare room his guffaw had the sound of wood being torn apart. 'For your records, I suppose?' His face lapsed back into embarrassed formality as he saw Cavers' shocked look. 'Pardon me,' Woolcott said.

Chapter Twenty-Nine

There was, for January, an unusual brightness in the sky. The days opened with a thin, golden mist through which the sun soon came. Small blue flowers appeared like the eyes of kittens among the ruins near the Wall and in the watchtowers the guards sat under the glass with their jackets off. If was as if winter had been rolled back a little with the retreat of the Russians. The swans on the Spree looked more relaxed and the delegates from Africa and the United Arab Republic seemed less reluctant to leave the girls of the Unter den Linden Hotel for the factory foremen of the official tours. At the *Opernbar* the industrial bosses and the Party chiefs drank German Scotch and clapped hands thunderously for the blonde singer. For the workers and their girls the string quartet in the Budapest Restaurant played melodies from some pre-war spring. Across the flatness of the divided city all the great landmarks of West Berlin stood high and near in the pure light – Mercedes, Hilton, Europa Center, Springer; almost touchable, it seemed, but still unreachable. For years they had been a torment. Now there was hope. There was hope, wasn't there? The East Berliners looked at each other as they asked. Eisler could feel the questioning. He had given them hope, now they were impatient for the reality.

Chapter Thirty

Karl Zetkin wore a grey light-weight suit, a cream coloured shirt and a green tie, for his meeting with Juliu Bahr at the Ministry of State Security. He, too, could hea the questioning; not just in the country, but in the Party not just about *Our Socialist Future*, but about his future.

As the Russians had withdrawn to bases in the country Zetkin's world had darkened; with fury at Eisler' successful defiance of Moscow; with regret at his ow timidity; with frustration at the recession of his dream: Being the handsomest man in the Praesidium, the bes dressed Communist of them all, was hardly enough.

Now, as Bahr explained the reason for the meeting sunbeams began to dance at the edge of Zetkin's darknes:

'The man's name is Derby,' Bahr was saying, his hea a little to the side as if one big ear weighed more than th other. 'He is an American spy. He was locked with Mr Sloane in a vault at the archives centre in Potsdam. Os tensibly, they were unknown to each other and were ther for the innocent purpose of examining documents relatin; to Nazi war crimes. Subsequently, they had lunch togethe in the Klosterkeller Hotel. Derby returned to Wes Berlin that same night and reported next morning to man called Woolcott, who operates an Imperialist spy ring from a base in Finckensteinallee.'

Zetkin's expression was a curiously tense mixture o pleasure and anger.

'It is outrageous,' he said hungrily. 'This must be liberalisation carried to the ultimate.' He slapped hi forehead. 'That we should have a First Secretary whe consorts with a woman who in turn consorts with American spies!'

Bahr wriggled a little on his pedestal seat, like an overgrown baby struggling with the nursery chair harness. 'I thought you would be disturbed,' he said moderately. 'Of course, if they were ordinary people I would have had them in prison by now. As it is . . .' he put a limp hand to his grey brow and looking almost appealingly at Zetkin '. . . I find it very worrying.'

'The law is the same for all of us,' Zetkin said with harsh enthusiasm. He looked at Bahr with sudden suspicion. 'How long have you known about this, Julius?'

'The report came to me yesterday morning. I confess I did not believe it. Last night I questioned the men involved. Unhappily, there can be no doubt.' He looked away to a table where the pornographic magazines of a few weeks ago were again assembled. *Don't Stop Or I'll Scream. Don't Scream Or I'll Stop.* Heinrich was still on the trail.

'Unhappily?'

'Of course,' Bahr said. 'It is a slur on the entire Government.'

Zetkin's look was uncaring. 'This meeting between Mrs Sloane and the American spy took place more than a week ago,' he persisted.

Bahr ignored the suggestion of inefficiency. 'Yes, the significance of the meeting was not appreciated. It was the man Derby who was under observation. His visit seemed unexciting until someone realised who Mrs Sloane was.'

'Where is Mrs Sloane now?'

'Still researching in Potsdam.'

Zetkin had the expression of a policeman reluctantly admiring the audacity of a master criminal. 'And Comrade Eisler?'

'Walter is here in Berlin, involved in a round of trivial

engagements. He appears to be trying to cool the tem
perature by giving the impression that the crisis is over
His diary for the next few days could not be less exciting

'I take it you will be arranging something of consequenc
for him, then, Julius?' Zetkin's manner was openly jovia
now. 'This should be a memorable day for the Ministr
of State Security.'

Bahr ran a hand over his desk. 'There could possibl
be some quite innocent explanation.'

Zetkin's joviality ended. 'It is up to you, Julius, to se
that there is no innocent explanation.' His voice wa
challenging. 'If you cannot stage the trial of your caree
out of this material then you should be in another Ministry
But if you act as you should, nothing will be too good fo
you. I can promise you that.' His manner had becom
lordly.

Bahr looked through the fingers of the hand on whicl
his head rested. His voice was sly. 'Are you handing ou
the laurels already, Karl?'

Zetkin adjusted his jacket and retreated a little
'Moscow will see that you are suitably rewarded. You
Ministry will have achieved with complete legality wha
could not be accomplished even with the threat of thirty
Red Army divisions.'

'And what would you consider to be a suitable reward.
Karl? For instance?' Bahr's look was old-fashioned and
inviting.

'I have told you, Julius. Nothing would be beyond you.'

Bahr slid quickly from his high chair. His voice rose.
'You must count me very simple. Apart from your own
well-known ambitions, the man who topples the throne
never sits on it. It is one of the great truths of politics.'

He began walking carefully round the edge of a carpet,
placing one foot neatly in front of the other, like a child
following the intricate design of a cracked paving stone.

When he was facing Zetkin he stopped. He looked fragile and bony.

'Walter Eisler and Margaret Sloane will be arrested,' he snapped, 'if and when I am directed to do so by a higher authority or when I can be persuaded that I am not acting alone. Or even worse . . .' the skin of his face tightened to tearing as he spat the words '. . . acting with you.'

Zetkin stared at him in astonishment. 'You have been pleased to act with me until now.'

'But now it would be improper. Now you are the subject of an inquiry under the Ordinance for the Security of the People's Republic.'

Zetkin looked transfixed. 'What is this?'

Bahr's stance became formal. 'You are well aware that Paragraph Nine was invoked against you by Walter Eisler. Accordingly, you may yourself shortly be the subject of what could be a memorable trial.'

It seemed that Zetkin was about to throw himself across the desk. 'You twisted little swine. You told me that . . .'

Bahr retreated till his hand hovered over a switch.

'You see, Karl,' he said, 'I would really much prefer that Eisler's trial be a Russian one. It would leave my hands clean. I could not then be reproached by those of our colleagues who presently share Eisler's dream.'

'You've got the bloodiest hands in the country,' Zetkin said.

Bahr bowed a little. 'I would not like to have to add your blood to the mixture, Karl. Therefore, I suggest you go to the Soviet Embassy and throw the first stone. Unless, of course, you would prefer that Eisler gets away with this.'

Zetkin's face was blotched with hate. He smashed his fist on to the desk. 'Do your own dirty work.'

'No, Karl. I want you to do it for me. And if you don't, there is the worrying question of these serious charges against you. I cannot shelve them forever. They may in the end be unprovable but an investigation would be ruinous for you. That would be distressing – and so needless.'

Strands of Zetkin's brown hair had tumbled over his forehead. 'You're mad, Julius,' he said.

Bahr seemed to consider this.

'You'll never be Chief of State,' Zetkin said.

When Zetkin had gone Bahr buzzed his secretary. His voice was low and courteous as if he was already clothed in a new and awesome authority. 'I would like,' he said, 'to speak to Comrade Albert Behrens.'

Chapter Thirty-One

Fräulein Kopf was wearing a fawn coloured coat with a high fur collar and wide fur trimming at the cuffs. Her sunglasses were rimmed with gilt. She looked poised, elegant and mysterious.

She said: 'There's another marriage bureau somewhere in Pankow, Freddi. I'm telling all the others to go there. Remind me to get the address for you.'

He made two or three impatient movements with his hands. 'No,' he said. 'I'll stay with you.'

'What's the use? I haven't found anyone for you. In a week or so I'll be gone, as soon as the divorce comes through.'

'But you said I could come.' His heart thumped at the enormity of his intention. 'Over there.'

'Well, you can come. I won't stop you. But you must think very carefully about it.'

It baffled him how she could be so matter-of-fact. After their first long talk about it she had never mentioned the tunnel again. He had come on his next visit certain that the bureau would be abandoned, but she had been sitting at her desk as usual apparently concerned only with the problem of finding a wife for him.

He said: 'What is there to think about?'

'For a start, why should you want to leave East Germany? You have a good job here. The system doesn't seem to worry you. I've never heard you say a word against it. Over there you'll be just another refugee.'

And what would she be? He was gripped by fear for her future. For a week or two she would be a heroine. For three months she had been sitting in this room, the last link in a chain along which sixteen political outlaws had hauled themselves to freedom. He could imagine the hulabaloo, the newspaper and television interviews when she arrived out of a hole in the ground in West Berlin, smiling at them with her beautiful white teeth. Then, the slow return to silence. No one ever remembered yesterday's hero.

'Never mind me,' he said. 'What will you do?'

She shrugged as if it didn't matter what she did.

'You could always open another marriage bureau,' he said.

She gave him a fond look and leaned forward on the desk with her arms folded in front of her. 'I doubt if I have a true vocation for that, Freddi. I tried. I really wanted to help people while I was here. I know what it is to be lonely . . . and unhappy, but . . . well, it didn't work out.'

Behind her, sunlight fought with the grime on the window.

Her bravery inspired him to impishness. 'Then what about another baby linen shop?'

She laughed and held up her hands. 'You've got big ideas for me, Freddi, but they take money, and I haven' any.'

'Oh, I could let you have some money,' he said. 'If it would help.'

He put a little away every week, like a dowry, but he felt now that he would never need it if all the world had to offer was a collection of Evas and Carlas, one standard model with unremarkable variations. He had been born a bachelor and he would die one . . . unless. He tried to stifle the impossible thought.

'Thanks for the offer, Freddi, but I really don't know what I want to do.'

'I don't know why you wait on here,' he said queru-lously. 'I've told you how dangerous it is. Your work is finished. Won't you leave to-day?' His voice had become pleading.

'No. I want the divorce. When I reach West Germany I want to be free in every way.'

A thin beam of light pierced the window and settled on her hair. The brown strands looked soft and warm. The cheap local scent reached him on a dusty line of sunshine. It wasn't good enough for her. He remembered the name on a bottle that he had seen Margaret using . . . Estee Lauder. That was what she should have. As soon as they reached West Berlin he would buy her the biggest bottle he could find.

She was saying something but he sat there thinking his own thoughts. Unless . . . unless . . . the preposterous thoughts would not be denied.

Eventually, he knew beyond doubt what he should do about Gerda Kopf but by then he was miles away.

He telephoned her from a public booth. 'I've got two tickets for *Marie Stuart* for to-morrow night,' he said hoarsely. 'Will you come?' He cringed at his dreadful bluntness.

The silence seemed unending. 'I couldn't, Freddi. I'm sorry.'

His sigh whistled down the line like a cold wind. 'I knew you wouldn't,' he said. 'I shouldn't have bothered you.'

'It's no bother, Freddi. That's not it, at all.'

'I'll post the tickets to you,' he said stoically. 'Perhaps you have a friend.' If he couldn't be successful at least he could be generous.

'You don't understand. It's the divorce. I don't want anything to go wrong. If we were seen together it might be bad for me.'

'Oh.' He smiled his relief into the cold instrument. 'Is that all? I could meet you in the street outside the theatre and leave you there, couldn't I? No one could make anything of that.'

'Well, I don't know.' She sounded worried, and perhaps not just for herself. 'Oh, all right. But Freddi?'

'Yes?'

'Just this once, until . . . until I'm free.'

The words came to him like a message of hope. Again he smiled into the telephone and then jerked up, startled, as a man with an angry face knocked on the glass. Comrade Zander said hurriedly, 'I'll see you to-morrow night, then.'

There was something extraordinarily solemn and binding about the quite ordinary words. As he came out of the box he felt that he had been participating in a ceremony during which he had taken some kind of vow which he might never fully understand and from which only death would release him.

He crunched his way along the street, through some sandstone debris that had spilled from behind a barricade. Another bit of Imperial Germany was being torn down to make way for Democratic Communist concrete. To-day he felt there was something symbolic about the gritty ruins. An era had ended. Freddi Zander was being redeveloped as well.

Chapter Thirty-Two

The old ceiling of the dimly-lit room showed dirty white above them as a vehicle turned at the end of the lane, its headlight beam moving slowly across the bedroom window like the prying ray of a prison camp spotlight.

Eisler closed his eyes, but the events of the day stayed there in front of him, sharp and clear in the darkness of his mind like statues floodlit for a festival.

'As if we hadn't enough,' he said, 'without you having lunch with an American spy.' For some reason that he wasn't quite sure about, but of which he was vaguely ashamed, he wanted to sound accusing and he kept staring at a stretch of unattractive blue wallpaper which looked as if it had been hung generations ago by someone who hated it.

She sighed. 'I know, but we mustn't go over it all again. You must get to sleep.'

The window shuddered in its old dry frame as a gust of wind struck the house. He listened for a while to the trees creaking and the leaves scurrying in the dark corners of the garden.

'God help me, Margaret,' he said with sudden sorrow, 'but for two or three minutes, this morning, I doubted you. The way Albert Behrens told it there seemed only one explanation.'

'I suppose that's how he wanted it to sound.'

'I suppose so.'

A door slammed somewhere in the house and he fancied

that he could hear the slippered feet of the old caretaker shuffling down one of the thinly-carpeted corridors.

'Anyway, let's stop talking about American spies.' Again his voice had become accusing.

She looked at him protestingly. 'You're the one who started it.'

'And now I want to stop it,' he said loudly.

'I think you're ill,' she said.

'Oh, God.'

'No, I do. Seriously.'

'Seriously ill?'

'You know what I mean, Walter. Don't pretend. It's a wonder you haven't cracked before this.'

He made a groaning sound against the pillow. 'Yes, I know what you mean.' He looked up almost furtively. 'Do you believe in God, Margaret?'

Even in the dimness he could see her surprise. She shook her head. 'Not in the way you mean.' She smiled slightly. 'But if it's any help, I believe in the Devil.'

He was silent for two or three seconds. 'If you believe in one you must surely believe in the other?'

'I don't think there is any other.'

'You mean you think the Devil created the world?'

'Well, doesn't it make more sense if you think of it that way?'

He had hoped for something comforting from her, but there was no comfort in this.

She said: 'Isn't it obvious that the Creator was supremely evil?'

His voice was baffled. 'I don't know, Margaret. It's only now I've started to think about these things.'

'Have you ever seen a man, or an animal, have a heart-attack, Walter? A fatal heart-attack that lasted about half an hour?'

'What's that got to do with it?'

184

'It's awful. If an ordinary man did anything as monstrous as that to his children we would rightly say he was evil. But all the time, all over the world, the Creator is doing things like that to us, his children, yet for him we find excuses. We support churches to propagate these excuses. In our desperation to blame it all on somebody else we created an evil entity called the Devil. But I believe there's only one entity, the one that we call God. And I believe he does it all, the good and the horrific.'

It wasn't what he had wanted. These days, the word *God* brought to his mind comforting images of red candles flickering warmly at the feet of benign statues in mellow churches. God was some sort of sanctuary. Come to me all ye who are heavy laden and I will give thee peace. He wanted a God who would ease his burden.

He said wearily: 'There must be a flaw in that argument.'

There had, he thought, been a flaw in everything he had ever encountered. In Marxism. In Leninism. In Albert Behrens. Where, he wondered miserably, was Margaret's flaw? He squirmed away in horror from the terrible thought.

'A long time ago that's what I thought, too,' Margaret said. 'I kept looking for the flaw. I wanted there to be one. I wanted to go on believing. There's so much comfort in believing.'

Her voice became lighter. 'You know, I don't believe you're a Communist at all, Walter. You shouldn't be worrying about God. Marx and Lenin did away with him for you. I had to get rid of him for myself.'

'Albert Behrens believes in God,' he said defensively. 'At least, I think he does. He told me he prays.'

'It hasn't done him much good. He's still rotten enough to be after your job.'

'At least he warned me of what's going on . . . about this man Derby. He didn't have to do that if all he wants is my job.'

'Maybe not. And then, maybe he had a guilty conscience.'

'I wish I could pray,' Eisler said. 'Once or twice recently I've tried, but I felt I was trying to get something for nothing.'

She drew his head on to her breast. 'My poor darling,' she said. 'You've nothing left now, have you?'

'Only you.' His breath was warm against her scented skin.

'And instead of comforting you, all I'm doing is scoring debating points. I've only added to your troubles.' Her arms tightened round him and her voice became fierce. 'If I ever see that man Derby again I'll push him under a bus.'

He pulled away from her in a sudden, invalid panic. 'Whatever happens, Margaret, you must get out of East Berlin, out of East Germany, to-morrow.' He twisted his watch round on his wrist and peered at it. 'To-day,' he said. 'You must get out to-day.'

'I won't go without you.'

It was an enormous effort even to argue with her. 'It's more important that you get out. I don't think they'll try anything against me, direct. The evidence is far too paltry.'

'Even for them?'

'Yes, even for them,' he said stubbornly, trying not to remember all the men he had known condemned on evidence no less paltry.

'Both of us or neither of us,' she said.

The slightly evil smell of decaying leaves wafted in coldly through the two or three inches of open window. The wind was still rising.

'I've told you before, Margaret. I'm not going to run away. Above all, not now. I held out against the Russians. 'm not going to be beaten by a poisonous dwarf like ulius Bahr.'

'Poisonous dwarfs sometimes succeed where bullying ;iants fail,' she said.

Chapter Thirty-Three

When Eisler wakened he was alone. There had been a heavy fall of snow and the drab room was bright with reflected light. He looked about in alarm until he saw and read Margaret's note. She had gone to Potsdam with Comrade Zander.

It was almost nine o'clock. They had argued until after three o'clock, when he had fallen into an exhausted sleep. He went to the window. The garden had in recent years been planted with young fir trees, the branches of which were now furry and indistinct under the new snow. Two wheel tracks went past the front of the house, curved round an ancient larch tree and disappeared. As he looked at the tyre pattern in the snow he was suddenly terrified that he might never see Margaret again. Julius Bahr's men might be waiting for her along the road. The note might not even be genuine. Perhaps they had been at the house while he slept and it was they who had taken her.

He hurried from the room and went through the rest of the house, not knowing what he was looking for, but fearful that he would find Comrade Zander lying somewhere with a bullet in him. He drew into a doorway as he heard footsteps, but it was only the old caretaker, nodding cheerfully at him as she passed carrying a mop and a bucket of steaming water. He went back, still uneasy, to the bedroom and had washed and dressed and was standing fretfully at the end of the lane when the car returned.

Margaret was wearing a suède coat and knee-high

boots. She was bare-headed and wore no gloves. He went to her eagerly.

As she saw his expression of relief she said: 'Didn't you see the note? I couldn't sleep and the morning was so beautiful. I heard Freddi getting the car out and went with him for the run.'

'Freddi?' He felt unreasonably puzzled. Anything even slightly out of the ordinary seemed to balloon swiftly towards the unmanageable. She was right. He must be ill.

'Yes.' She nodded towards the car. 'Freddi Zander.'

'Of course.' He felt ashamed that he had never taken more interest in the man.

The sun had come out and the vast, receding landscape of distant houses and tall trees looked safe and friendly. Last night he had been afraid that by this time the house would be surrounded. Now, the possibility seemed remote and ridiculous. He turned to the bodyguard and said casually: 'Were there many people about?'

Comrade Zander's gaze was steady and unsurprised. 'There were some children playing in the snow. I don't think we saw another car after leaving Potsdam.' He turned to Margaret as if for confirmation but she was looking over and beyond him.

When she had made the coffee and they were sitting at the window, drinking it, Eisler said: 'I want you to leave to-day for the West, Margaret. The more I think about that American the less I think they could make of your meeting with him. But they might try. You needn't go any further than West Berlin. In a month or so the situation here will be different. The tension will fall when they realise that I'm not going to rush at things. I've learned that much.

'The Wall can't come down overnight. The first thing I'm going to do is get rid of censorship. We will see what happens then.'

189

He was surprised at the change in her attitude. She was almost submissive. He had expected her to start protesting again but she merely nodded and said: 'All right, Walter. I'd rather stay and see this out with you but I can see I'm only another worry. I'll go to-morrow.'

'To-day,' he said quickly, fears rising in him that were too vague and fleeting to be properly identified.

'No. To-morrow. I've got all sorts of things to do. Remember, I came here to work. I've got notebooks and other material to collect from the archives centre. I want to be able to start writing when I leave.'

He closed his mind to the unnameable fears. 'I suppose to-morrow will have to do, then.' He looked at his watch and gulped down the last of his coffee. 'I'll have to go. There's a meeting of the Praesidium at noon.'

She took his arm and walked him to the door. 'I'll have a meal ready for you.'

'No. I don't know how late I might be. Perhaps very late.'

'It doesn't matter. I'll make something that won't spoil.' She smiled and pressed his arm. 'I'd like to.'

Words from the encroaching world of religious belief came into his head: *The Last Supper*. He spoke them in an ironic tone of voice.

Her hold on his arm tightened. 'Don't say that.'

He bent and kissed her and then put his arms tightly around her. 'If only we were two ordinary people.'

She leaned away as if to see him better. 'I love you, Walter,' she said. 'I really love you.' Her voice was hoarse and she was almost in tears.

Chapter Thirty-Four

She waited until Eisler had been gone for about an hour and then telephoned to Potsdam for a taxi. By lunch-time she was in East Berlin at the checkpoint in Fried-richstrasse Station. By S-bahn, West Berlin was only half a mile away. She had looked up Wipperstrasse, where Derby lived. Zoological Garden was the nearest station. The eighty-six pfennig return ticket was in her purse.

Now the guard was holding her passport. He said with faint accusation: 'This is you?'

She smiled uneasily. 'Of course.'

'It is not a good likeness.'

When the guards wanted to be awkward, or were suspicious, trains came and went and an anxious or bored traveller could sit for a very long time on the wooden benches. It was best to be helpful.

'Perhaps it's my hair,' she said. 'I wore it a bit longer and swept back a bit more at the sides when that picture was taken.'

'You are breathless, Fräulein,' he said. 'Have you been running?'

Her heart thumped. 'Yes. For the train.'

'There are many trains.'

He was squinting, trying to see both her face and the photograph at once.

'The styles change so often,' she said.

He looked at her over the passport. He was about thirty and his eyes were surly. 'In America?'

She spread her hands and smiled helplessly, 'Most places, I suppose.'

'Not in the Deutsche Demokratische Republik,' he said flatly.

Was he proud of the fact or did he resent it? 'The girls are very smart here,' she said tactfully.

'I am married,' he murmured as if that kept him from noticing what the girls looked like. He was still fingering the passport. 'When was this picture taken?'

A loudspeaker crackled and as a voice recited a list of numbers two or three men rose from the benches and went to a window to collect their papers.

She wondered with a feeling of chill if her name had been circulated to the checkpoints. Were they going to stop her leaving? Was this talk about the photograph an excuse to keep her there until someone more senior arrived? Or was the guard simply being obstructive?

'It was taken fairly recently,' she said. 'Look,' she added desperately, 'does this help?' She pulled her hair behind her ears into a semblance of the style in the photograph.

He grinned at the pose and turned from the photograph to the page stamped with her entry visa. He glanced at the ground round about her and said: 'You have no luggage?'

'No. I'll be back in two or three hours.'

He frowned. 'Then you must have a day exit visa.' He flicked the open passport with his forefinger. 'When you cross the border this visa terminates. With only this you will not be allowed to return East at night. There would be a delay.'

Delays, she thought with sudden fury, are what you specialise in here. Words of resentment at the system threatened to flow from her. She had so much that was so important to do. She was trying to save the man she loved. She lit a cigarette to control her anger.

She said: 'Can you give me a day visa?'

He shook his head with a suggestion of bureaucratic triumph. 'The nearest place is in Hans Beimler Strasse. There is a Reiseburo office there next to the Volkspolizei Headquarters.'

For *next*, she thought, substitute *attached to*. Tourism and police supervision were inseparable in this country.

She said: 'But that's miles away. I'm in a hurry.'

He handed back her passport as if he had not heard. 'The charge is only fifteen Marks.' He sounded slightly wistful and she realised that he, too, was a prisoner. The guards were the ones with the worst temptation. They had the highest escape rate of any class and were allowed to patrol only in pairs. Since the Wall was built almost three thousand had defected.

She turned frustratedly away and went to find a taxi. The country, she thought, was strangled in restrictions. Supervision had become a way of life. She remembered her disbelief when she had discovered that visitors even needed a visa to travel about inside the country. She had required an additional permit to go the short distance from Berlin to Potsdam.

As she sat on the inevitable bench at the Reiseburo she realised the growing depth of her dislike for the Socialist State. And yet, that was the way the whole world was going. Whatever they called themselves, politicians everywhere were bringing the people within ever-increasing State control. Big Brother was no longer a slur to be flung only at Communist countries. All Governments were busily undermining human liberty. How long, she wondered, before even the United States was run on Socialist principles? The pink men were already there in huge numbers. In Britain, these days, every Government was Socialist.

She rose hurriedly from the slatted bench as a shirt-sleeved official waved her passport at her from the counter.

*

A grey, snow-laden twilight had settled on West Berlin when she reached Wipperstrasse after a taxi run from the railway station through streets that seemed dangerously congested after the empty stretches on the other side of the Wall.

The address Derby had given her was a modern block of service flats. He was out.

'Can you give me his business address?' she asked as the porter put the telephone down. 'It's very important.'

The man took out a book and consulted a list. He shook his head. 'There is no other address given.' As he saw her expression he added: 'But Mr Derby is always in for a little while around half-past-five.

It was just on three-thirty. 'I'll come back,' she said. 'Tell him Margaret Sloane called.' She scribbled the name on a pad.

The streets were damp and in the Kurfurstendamm she went into a crowded cafe. These were free Berliners and it could be no illusion, she told herself, that they looked happier than the other ones. Why were the lights always dimmer, the shops and streets emptier, the faces sadder, the clothes drabber in the Communist heavens? Were these things absolutely inseparable from the system? The books were unreadable and the films did not entertain. Why? No one had ever been able to tell her. She had never managed to make even Walter fully appreciate the awful, crushing dullness of what was supposed to be a revolution and a crusade. Perhaps it would be seen eventually as one of history's great contradictions.

As she lifted her cup she realised with a tremor of fright that a man two or three tables away was watching her. He had come into the cafe after her. As their eyes met his gaze drifted slowly to another part of the cafe. There was something very expert about the way he disengaged his eyes. He was about fifty, with limp brown hair combed forward, Caesar-style, as if to conceal baldness. His raincoat fitted peculiarly closely, as if he was so rarely without it that it had become part of him. He was broadly built and at least of medium height but something about him made her think of Comrade Zander. Here was a man with the same patient expression, the same long-suffering eyes that Eisler had described as vacant but which were to her expressive of a mind introverted by long periods of loneliness. This was the face of another watcher and waiter.

She rose almost without thought and walked into the street. There was a traffic hold-up and, again without thinking, she plunged through the maze of vehicles. A last panicky backward glance showed her two empty tables; her own and the one at which the man had been sitting.

She walked quickly in the direction that she happened to be pointing, but gradually the panic subsided. Did it matter if someone was following her? She had probably been followed everywhere for the past two months. All that really mattered was that she should be successful in what she had come to do. It wouldn't matter if Julius Bahr secured additional evidence of a link between her and Derby. They could hardly make use of the information in any less than twenty-four hours. And by then it would be too late. She was seized by an enormous wish that she could regain enough faith to pray, to be able to say something simple, like *Pray God, by then it will be too late.* She was ashamed that she had mocked Eisler for his questions about God. She had no right to impose her spiritual desolation on him.

She stopped at the window of a restaurant that seemed to specialise in soup. Kraftbruhe, Huhnerbruhe, Koniginsuppe, Gulaschsuppe, Zwiebelsuppe, Ochsenschwanz-Suppe, Tomatensuppe, Schildkrotensuppe.

She turned quickly from the menu to look along the street. There was no sign of the man in the raincoat. Perhaps he hadn't been following her. When you were as unnerved as she was to-day the imagination could go berserk. She began to remind herself of other times when she had been frightened. In Washington, when she had been trapped in a doorway during a march of militant Negroes. Over a jungle in Biafra when the helicopter she was in had developed engine trouble and the pilot had brought it thumping down in a clearing after a terrifying descent on the auto-rotating blades. There had been bomb incidents in Saigon.

She crossed the street again and passed the ruin of the Kaiser-Wilhelm-Gedachtniskirche and beside it the modern concrete replacement. People would be praying in the queer blue interior of the new church. She envied them the comfort of their faith. When she reached the Europa Center an icy draught was swirling through the wide arcades. There was music playing and she followed the sound until she came to a floodlit ice rink where children were skating. Smiling parents leaned on the rail, holding coats. The music was gay and everyone looked very happy. It added to the unreality. She went through another arcade and on to the open street. The pavement became less busy as she reached the perimeter of the shopping area. Homegoing traffic was coming out of a tunnel at high speed and branching into the lanes that led to suburban Berlin. For most of these people, she thought, the evening would be uneventful. Another crisis of the Wall had passed and for them the future career of Walter Eisler was something to be awaited with interest but without alarm.

Brakes screeched as the pedestrian light flashed in her

favour. She crossed. On this side of the street there were no shops. The pavement was lit only by high overhead lamps and the flash of car headlights. Ahead, she could see the Hilton Hotel. On the twelfth floor the Roof Garden waiters would be laying the tables for dinner. Three minutes would take her to the apartment block where Derby lived. She was still too early. She stopped, half amused at her panicstricken dash along the Kurfurstendamm. At least, by luck, it had been in the right direction.

Beside her there was a short flight of steps leading to a glass door above which there was a sign: FISH AND REPTILES. The zoo must be nearby and these were some of the neighbours that she had thought so appropriate for Derby. She started to smile, but something about the dark, snow-threatened street made her feel sick and cold again. This, she thought, is fear. She was afraid of what she planned to do and afraid that she might in the end not have the courage to do it. A middle-aged woman and three or four laughing children came through the glass doors and down the steps. In there it would be bright and warm. She went up to the cash desk.

'We will be closing soon,' the woman said.

'It doesn't matter.' She pushed the admission charge further forward. Another party of school children jostled her on their way out.

She took the first corridor that she saw and walked past batteries of glass insect cases where poisonous-looking shapes darted out of miniature caves with tongues flicking and wings whirring, through brightly-lit rooms with glass walls behind which bloated shadows glided. She hadn't bought a catalogue and the names on the tanks meant little to her. It was ridiculous, she thought, even being in a place like this at such a time. It seemed an essential part of the human fate to be rendered absurd even in times of tragedy. Grotesque and comic human images came back to her from Nigeria and Vietnam. She banished them, shuddering, and looked about in faint surprise at finding herself back in the entrance hall. She had completed a circle of the ground floor at almost laughable speed, illustrating her own theory of the bathos lurking in all human stress.

A broad staircase rose to a landing and then branched both ways. She climbed it, taking the left turn. Two uniformed attendants passed her on their way down.

'We will be closing soon,' one of them said.

She nodded. The turning she had chosen led into what looked like a vast conservatory. She stopped at the entrance, startled by a long, high-pitched screech that changed in tone and volume until it became a choking squawk.

Shsheeeawowaweegaw.

The sound was strangulated and vaguely human and it took her a second or two to realise it was made by a bird.

Damp heat engulfed her as she stepped inside. In the jungle of tropical shrubs and swaying creepers another bird shrieked. She peered into the shadows. Perhaps it was only a tape being played to heighten the drama.

There were snakes behind glass and in pits. At her feet, bubbles plopped in a muddy pool and a toothy trap of a mouth hissed and groaned at her and then sank back into the man-made swamp.

Shsheeeawowaweegaw.

Two girls passed with their fingers to their ears as the horrible bird call came again. Apart from the attendants, the girls were the only people she had seen on this floor.

The humidity was unpleasant but ahead she could see a hump-backed bridge. She hesitated and then went towards it. While she was here she might as well see the lot. It would be twenty minutes yet before Derby was home.

198

The bridge was constructed of branches lashed together with creeper to enhance the setting and as she stepped on to it she imagined it swaying over a ravine somewhere up the Amazon. She stopped as another grotesque cry went jarring through her. Then, as she looked down, she caught her breath. She was standing over a pool filled with alligators. Or were they crocodiles? Or giant iguanas? She never found out. As she turned away with vague horror to look for a notice she heard footsteps. When she turned again she saw the man with the Caesar haircut coming towards her.

He was walking on his heels as if to keep from toppling forward. She saw at a glance that she would not get past him. She looked round. There were no attendants or visitors in sight. Her mouth opened but her throat was dry and it was the hidden bird that supplied the sound.

Shsheeeawowaweegaw.

The man stopped as if frightened. She gulped at the hot, damp air and ran stumbling from the bridge into the shrub-grown depths on the far side.

Her heart was hammering and she wanted to be sick. Two or three narrow, curving paths led into another steamy plantation. She ran down one of them with snakes and lizards peering at her from behind cunningly concealed barriers. Her ankles ached and her handbag felt like a weight. Instinctively, she gripped it by the straps for use as a weapon.

She glanced repeatedly over her shoulder as she ran, stumbling against rocks and trees, then lurching on again.

Abruptly, its circle completed, the path came back to where it started and she was again facing the hump-backed bridge. But where was the man? Following her? Or waiting, knowing that she must return this way?

Shsheeeawowaweegaw.

Her heart jumped. A two-second dash would take her

199

over the bridge. Another five or six seconds and she could be on the main staircase within calling distance of the attendants. But if he was waiting for her he might shoot her before she was half-way across.

Other possibilities crowded in. It might be a knife he had. Or a hypodermic. A gas spray . . .

At that moment he came out of a path on her right. She swung her handbag in his direction in a feeble threatening gesture. At the same time she started backing towards the bridge. In a strange way the confrontation strengthened her. There was no room now for imagination. He was no more than twelve feet away and a narrow beam of make-believe sunlight was playing on him through a gap in the foliage.

He was moving forward, as if mesmerised, at the same speed as she was edging backwards. The Caesar haircut ended on his forehead in a ragged edge that coarsened his face. His mouth opened and he said something that she was too frightened to hear. His hand stretched towards her as if inviting her to surrender.

No more than ten seconds had passed since he came out of the path. Now, his hand still out, he charged at her; awkwardly, as if thrown forward by an uncontrollable nervous spasm.

She felt her hand pulling back and then she was flinging the handbag hard at his face. As the heavy brass clasp struck him, he stopped as if he had hit a wall. Then, moaning, he swayed blindly past her, moving backwards with short, tottering steps. His hands covered his face and blood trickled from between his fingers.

She watched, stupefied, as his agonised backward shuffle took him on to the bridge. His heel caught in one of the open slats, throwing him against the waist-high parapet. His feet left the ground and moved slowly upwards until he was stretched almost straight out with the small of his back on the parapet. His hands came away from his face and clawed at the air. His legs kicked. Then, as the point of balance was lost, he slid over.

Shsheeeawowaweegaw.

He landed with his legs in a muddy pool and lay quite still as two or three scaly shapes appeared from a group of rocks and began moving purposefully towards him on short thick legs.

Chapter Thirty-Five

The sitting-room of Derby's flat was small and furnished with the kind of anonymous teak that Margaret hated. To-night she hardly noticed. What she was grateful for was the reassurance of Derby's American voice.

'I wish I knew who he was,' she said for the third or fourth time. 'At first I thought he'd followed me from East Berlin, but if he had he wouldn't have attacked me.' She looked at Derby, as to an expert, for confirmation.

Derby avoided her eyes and handed her a large drink.

'Maybe he wasn't meant to attack you. Maybe he was simply incompetent and panicked.'

'He said something, but I couldn't make it out. I don't think it was in German.'

Derby picked up a woodcarving from Oberammergau. Everyone in the bureau had a collection of them. If they felt they were being followed they went into the gift shop instead of going upstairs.

An enormous loathing of Woolcott and his grandiose machinations rose in him. 'You don't seem to realise, Mrs Sloane,' he said unsteadily, guilt thickening his voice, 'that every intelligence service in Europe will be taking an interest in you. This guy might even have been a freelance.'

She looked puzzled.

'Berlin, both sides,' he said, 'is stacked up with would-be secret agents, all hoping to turn up something that will win them the jackpot.' Woolcotts, he thought bitterly. Scores of Woolcotts. Unofficial, unsuccessful, but filled with the same dark dreams as Woolcott.

She shuddered on the vodka. 'If I didn't know better I might think you were a bunch of romantic crackpots.'

Derby still had on his long black coat. Under the coat he wore a grey scarf crossed over his chest. It hid his collar and tie. She was reminded of photographs of reception committees standing on Russian airfields. He looked oddly Slavonic, she thought, to be an American spy. Perhaps that was one of his qualifications.

Derby put down the woodcarving as if it was a chess man. 'In this business,' he said, 'one of the first things you have to learn is that you can never count on making sense of very much.'

She tried to blot out a picture of dark, leathery creatures hurrying towards the fallen man. 'Whoever he was working for he's probably dead by now,' she said.

Derby brightened a little. 'Either that,' he said, 'or someone's going to be left with a one-legged spy.'

He took off his coat and threw it over a spindly writing-desk. He looked at her as candidly as his conscience would let him.

'Anyway, it looks as if that trip of mine to Potsdam wasn't wasted after all.'

Now that the moment had come to speak, the enormity of her intention overwhelmed her. She had to fight against the labouring of her heart. She looked at Derby yearningly and said:

'If Walter Eisler crossed to West Berlin would you . . . I mean, your people . . . see that nothing happened to him?'

He stared at her for two or three seconds as if he had not understood and then, turning away without speaking, began pouring himself another drink.

'He wouldn't be putting himself in your hands, or anything like that,' she said hurriedly. 'There isn't any deal. I just want to know if you would be willing to fly him some place out of the way. Lisbon, perhaps.'

Derby was unable to hide his agitation. His voice was suspicious.

'Are you telling me Eisler wants to defect?'

Her reaction was vicious. 'He doesn't want to defect. Men like that don't defect. He probably wouldn't even speak to anyone like you. That's what I meant when I said there's no deal.'

'Then I don't understand.'

'You told me in Potsdam that your people don't like what he's proposing to do. If you do what I'm asking his proposals will never be carried out, because he won't be there. But that's all. You get nothing else out of it. There won't be any dancing publicity bear.'

After the wear and tear of the day, the vodka was making her light-headed and vulnerable. She supposed he had poured them as big as he dared.

He looked solemn, almost priestly, with the scarf crossing his chest like part of a vestment. 'You're seriously telling me that Eisler is ready to walk out?'

Her eyes filled with tears. 'He doesn't know anything about it. I'm going to bring him out.'

'If he doesn't know about this . . .' Derby made a sceptical face '. . . idea, how do you know you can persuade him?'

'I won't try to persuade him. I'll drug him. That's why I've come to you. There are drugs like that, aren't there?'

There was no longer any reality. The words didn't mean what they said. Walter, she thought desperately, I love you.

Unreality of an equal intensity began churning in Derby, for suddenly he knew that Margaret was serious. He felt sick as he thought of Woolcott's arrangements.

'Drugging him would be no problem,' he said, 'but how are you going to get him through the Wall?'

'Someone who is sympathetic knows a way. There is a tunnel.'

'You can trust this person?'

'He suggested it. He knew I was desperate to get Walter out of the country.'

'I asked if you can trust him?'

'I'm going to trust him.'

Derby made a movement with his hands to indicate that he hoped she knew there was a difference. For some reason that he could not fully understand he wanted Eisler to go on living. Was it just to spite Woolcott? He began to picture Woolcott's face when he told him that Eisler was coming out alive. That Cavers wasn't needed now.

He said: 'You'll have to tell all this to my boss to-morrow.'

She jumped from her seat. 'To-morrow won't do. You don't understand the urgency. I want you to get me something to-night. You must have experts on that kind of thing.'

'Now, wait a minute, Mrs Sloane. When is this going to happen?'

'To-morrow morning.'

'Christ!' He was looking at her with what seemed to be wonder. 'And all you need is the right drug? Everything else is fixed?'

'Yes. But I must get back to Potsdam to-night.'

He made another face. 'I admired you even in Vietnam, when your prying was a damned nuisance to us.' He was seeing her for the first time as someone fragile and almost beautiful. Could Woolcott get the sort of drug she needed? And if he couldn't, what would happen to her when Cavers started firing? Where would she be at the time?

He said: 'Do you go around with Eisler much . . . in

205

public, I mean?' Woolcott would kill him if he could hea
this.

She looked at him without understanding.

He could hint no further. 'I mean,' he said, 'you're saf
over here in West Berlin. You needn't go back East.'

She looked as if she was going to be angry but befor
she could speak he said: 'But I guess not!' He tucked hi
scarf in and reached for his coat. 'Are you going to marry
him?'

She turned away and sank down into a chair with
her hands covering her face.

Chapter Thirty-Six

For a moment, Woolcott looked almost frightened, but
when he spoke his voice was assured.

'There is no way now of calling Cavers off.'

'There must be some way,' Derby muttered, knowing
that there was no way.

'There are no telephones to East Berlin. Even if there
were, we couldn't use them. I don't have Cavers at the
end of a walkie-talkie. That leaves one possibility.' Woolcott smiled slightly but his lips seemed tight and hard to
move. 'Someone could go over there and try to find
Cavers. How about you, Ramsden? Would you like to
volunteer?'

'You know bloody well I can't go back there now. You
saw to that.'

Woolcott wet a finger with his tongue and smoothed
one eyebrow with it. 'It would be a hopeless task, anyway,'
he said reflectively.

'You don't know where Cavers is . . . or . . . when it's
going to happen, then?'

There was still a false note somewhere in Woolcott's
elaborate calm.

'Neither where nor when, Ramsden, except that it will
be at the moment of earliest convenience. I merely
pressed the button that opened the trap. How the dogs
run is out of my control.'

'If only you'd waited. Getting Eisler out of there alive
would really have been a feather in our cap.'

'I'm not looking for cap feathers,' Woolcott said in-
dignantly. 'It's Peace I'm interested in.' He seemed to

summon a burst of almost defiant determination from somewhere. 'And even it was possible to call the thing of I'd take a lot of convincing before I'd be deflected by these . . . ravings . . . of a hysterical girl.' He glared a Derby as if his intelligence had been insulted.

'She's serious.'

'She may be serious, but can she do it?'

'I don't know, but I can't just go back and tell her we're not interested in her scheme.'

'Oh, no. I'll get you the dope she wants from Kleve all right. We owe her that for making the journey.'

'And what good will it do her?'

For a moment Woolcott did not answer. He turned away. 'It'll keep her happy,' he said. He looked at his watch. 'Kleve should be at his rooms for another half-hour. I'll walk round there now.'

'I'll come with you.'

'No,' Woolcott said quickly. 'Get back and keep the girl company. I'll join you after I've seen Kleve.'

Chapter Thirty-Seven

At Woolcott's suggestion Margaret went back by way of Checkpoint Charlie and despite another heart-thumping delay, then a long wait for a taxi, she was in Potsdam more than an hour before Eisler.

To her surprise he was alert and excited. The gloom and worry of the morning seemed to have been shed.

'Progress at last,' he said with an enthusiasm that made her macabre preparations seem even more night-marish. 'We have fixed a date for the end of censorship. It is a start. It has been a profitable day.'

He was like a broker home from the City and she knew that to-night they were in different worlds. She could hardly now remember the details of *Our Socialist Future*. What she did remember seemed so commonplace that it was difficult to see how it had aroused so much fury. It was concerned with elementary human rights that should be taken for granted. She could see that this had been his preoccupation all day, not the danger of his own situation. One good and, probably, misleading meeting and he was back again in the land of hope.

Her own hope, she realised, was now pitifully limited. She didn't care any more about the East Germans. It meant little to her now that they might never again know what freedom meant. Her only hope was that she could get Eisler to West Berlin and then to Lisbon, or wherever it turned out to be, before anything happened to him. When she had achieved that, hope for her would end. She would have saved his life and killed his career. He would never be able to go back. No one would believe he had been taken out unwillingly. Even if they did believe it, in two or three days' absence everything would change. Someone else, Bahr, Behrens, Zetkin – what did it matter? – would be in control. The Russians would see to that.

She watched him rummaging among the bottles and wondered what kind of life it would be for him . . . afterwards. The thought was too frightening to sustain. All she knew, achingly, was that she must save him physically. She would lose him, but at least she would know he was alive and at liberty.

He found the bottle he was looking for and turned, holding it up questioningly. Then, when he saw her face, he put the bottle down and took her hand, shaking it a little as if to recall her.

'Are you all right, Margaret? You look . . . I don't know. Peculiar.'

She blinked herself back into the room. 'I'm tired,' she said. 'I'll be glad when to-morrow's over.' At least that was a statement of truth among the lies and deceptions. 'After all, I'm not looking forward to leaving you here.'

He crossed to the window and pulled the curtain as if unprepared to face to-morrow to-night. 'I hope it doesn't snow again,' he said. He came back, put a log on the fire and stood looking about the room. 'I suppose you managed to collect all your stuff together? I tried to telephone two or three times, but I couldn't get a reply.'

'I've had a busy day,' she said guiltily, 'but I'm all set now. It's amazing how much extra luggage I've collected.'

'The riches of the East,' he said, surprising and torturing her yet again with his buoyancy. 'Where will you stay over there?' He smiled at a distant memory of the area on the other side of the Wall. 'It's a pity I'm not going, too.' He said it as if Berlin was an ordinary city and the short journey was quite possible for him. 'I'd like to see the shops in the Ku'dam again.'

She was engulfed in heartbreak. She longed to cry against his cheek, to say: 'Oh, my darling, you are coming. You are.' Ridiculously, she remembered the long list of soups in the window of the restaurant in the Kurfürsten-damm. Huhnerbruhe for two, she said to herself, making it sound in her head like something at the end of a rainbow. She remembered the promise he had made, years ago it seemed, now, on the afternoon of their happy stroll in the Potsdam woods. 'It is even more beautiful here in spring-time when all these shrubs are in flower. We will come again on the first warm day of spring.' She had forgotten the scene and she would never see it again but she knew that she would remember the words for the rest of her life.

She forced herself to speak normally. 'Don't let's talk about to-morrow, Walter. Pour your drink while I go and see about the food.'

She went past the kitchen to Comrade Zander's room. The door was open and he was sitting on the edge of a chair as if waiting. 'You were successful, Mrs Sloane?'

Successful? What kind of success was it to have acquired the horrible, chemical means of robbing a man of his future?

'Yes,' she said plaintively, 'but can't we do it to-night? I want to get it over with. I can't go on acting naturally much longer.'

Comrade Zander looked surprised. 'At night in the area of the Wall the Vopos are very active, Mrs Sloane. At three o'clock in the morning the car would almost certainly be stopped.' He shook his head. 'No. We must stick to the routine, leaving here at the normal time. Morning is best, when the streets are busy.'

Chapter Thirty-Eight

She passed the night between nightmare wakefulness and uneasy stupor. Eisler's confidence had flooded her with new doubts. Was her analysis of the situation wrong after all? Was the crisis really over and the danger past? She couldn't believe that it was. The whole course of Communist politics was against Eisler. His own returning optimism was suspect. His judgment was warped by unreasonable hope, the hallucination of a man in a desert who keeps seeing water. He was obsessed and he was ill. He couldn't survive. He might even be acting, playing down the danger so that she would get out of the country with a minimum of fuss. It was even possible that he had done a deal with them, trading his future for her safety.

All her reasoning led her back to the conviction that he was as vulnerable as ever. If Julius Bahr didn't get him the Russians would. Someone would. She remembered something that Derby had said at their first meeting in Potsdam. 'The temperature in this part of the world wasn't too bad until a month or so ago, Mrs Sloane. Now it's gone pretty damned cold.' That was the moment when she had realised that Eisler was an abandoned man, that the West didn't want a liberalised East Germany, either. With painful concentration she went back over her talk with Derby in West Berlin the previous night and at the end she knew that nothing had changed. Derby had moved about among his awful teak furniture showing disbelief, suspicion and finally a cautious excitement, but there hadn't been a single word from him to suggest that Eisler should stay where he was and go on fighting for all the things that Derby's political masters were supposed to believe in.

As morning came she deliberately fought against sleep, feeling that to escape willingly for even an instant would be the final betrayal. If she couldn't keep watch in the final hours of this Gethsemane then she was a poor disciple.

It was just after nine o'clock when she put the capsule that Derby had given her into Eisler's second cup of coffee and went trembling out of the room, unable to answer something he said, swept by a queer hope that he might not drink the coffee. If he didn't, she would accept it as a sign. A sign from where? From the God that she did not believe in?

It was snowing again and she stood shaking at the kitchen window until she heard the door behind her open. She whirled hopefully with the racing blood clouding her eyes, ready to throw herself into his arms, babbling it all out.

It was Comrade Zander, pink from a recent shave but oddly lethal-looking in tightly-belted black leather coat and black beret. His body looked taut and his eyes were alert. She was reminded of Major Yepishev standing in the other room prodding Eisler off to Moscow. Here, suddenly, was another conqueror from the propaganda posters; soldier, sailor, space-traveller; man-made and, when the conditions were right, ready for anything.

'Is everything ready?' There was, she thought, an underglow of happiness shining through his surface concern. Fulfilment came in some funny ways.

'No,' she said shortly. 'I mean, it's too soon to look yet. They said ten minutes.'

'But you have been here for almost twenty minutes, Mrs Sloane. I heard you leave the other room.'

'Then you go,' she said chokingly. 'I couldn't.'

213

He went without another word. She waited for a while and then, dreading what she might see, forced herself to follow.

Eisler was unconscious. He had moved from the table to an armchair at the fire as if he had felt sleep coming on. She knelt beside him and pressed one of his hands to her cheek. He was warm and limp, like a relaxed animal. She had imagined that it would be frightening, but his appearance was reassuring. She marvelled at how simple it had been. She hadn't known exactly what to expect but had imagined furniture being knocked over, even the danger of him injuring himself if he fell. Obviously he hadn't even felt suspicious. If the rest of it went as smoothly as this . . .

Comrade Zander had gone out of the room but now he was standing beside her again holding Eisler's coat. They put it round him like a cloak and then manhandled him out of the house and into the back of the car.

The effort left her faint and breathless. She leaned against the car with the snow driving into her. 'He's so heavy,' she gasped. 'When we get to the tunnel . . . how will we manage? It'll be a long way.'

'He is a big man, but we will manage,' Comrade Zander said briskly. 'We will wrap him in something and drag him after us. It won't be a Reiseburo tour, but it is the only way.'

As he saw her begin to cry he handed the car keys to her. 'Will you drive, Mrs Sloane? I will be able to handle Comrade Eisler better. He must look as if he is sitting.'

When they were ready, Eisler was propped quite straight in the centre of the bench seat, his head tilted slightly forward as if he was sleeping or reading. Comrade Zander was between him and the nearside door, his head about a foot lower and his supporting arms somewhere round Eisler's back.

The car moved off with a flailing rattle that jerked Margaret's foot off the accelerator and on to the brake.

'It's only the snow chains,' Comrade Zander said. 'I put them on when I saw the weather.'

As she turned the car on to the Potsdam road she had a momentary glimpse of another car parked on the verge. It was facing in the direction that she had to take and it was almost buried in snow except for the windscreen. The wipers were on although the absence of tyre tracks suggested that the car had been there for a long time.

Two or three bends further on her heart jumped. The car that had been parked was now behind. Lumps of snow were sliding from the bonnet and from the roof, giving it the appearance of something rearing up out of an icecap.

'We're being followed,' she said and was surprised that she did not feel more frightened.

As she accelerated she glanced back to see how Comrade Zander was taking the news. There was a gun in his hand and he had twisted round to the rear window. Eisler had toppled sideways.

'It's an English Rover,' Comrade Zander said.

For a moment or two she was ridiculously comforted by this information. Perhaps they were only tourists. But parked on a January morning in heavy snow on a secondary road?

Before she could think any more about it the first shot came from Cavers' minimum recoil, high muzzle-velocity, low trajectory rifle. The bullet entered by the back window and went out through the front, showering the inside of the car with a hailstorm of safety glass. The car swerved as she lowered her head. She fought the urge to take her hands from the wheel to cover her face. When she looked up a forest of pine trees was rushing towards her, dark avenues capped with fluffy pyramids of snow.

There was another shot, much closer this time, and she

realised it was from Comrade Zander's gun. She wrenched the wheel hard to the right and brought the car churning back through the soft snow to its own side of the road.

Comrade Zander's gun roared again. The driving mirror was still intact and in it she saw that they had drawn away from the Rover. She had a confused impression of someone in a soft hat leaning out of the other car.

'Faster,' Comrade Zander shouted. 'They don't have snow chains. Faster.'

She put the accelerator down as far as it would go. The car slid sickeningly, righted itself and shot forward. She heard three more quick rifle shots and then the car stopped going forward and started tearing across the road in a screeching sideways lurch. She lost her grip on the steering. The noise was terrible and the direction of the car kept changing as it hit various objects. Then it was bouncing down a steep slope, rolling over and over as it went. She felt no fear and no pain. She felt herself leaving the car and flying over the snow. There was a burst of orange flame as the petrol tank caught fire. Then she hit something hard.

Comrade Zander was also thrown from the car. He landed softly in a clump of bushes and lay dazed and gasping on his back. When he crawled into the open the snow was alive with candle flames of fire from the showering petrol. Near him, the lower branches of a tree were black and smouldering. Further down the slope he saw what was left of the car. Smoke was drifting from it but there was no flame. He stumbled to it down a steaming track of gouged up snow and earth. There wasn't much left except a lattice work of buckled and melted metal. Eisler's blackened body was still inside. Comrade Zander vomited and then began crawling round the wreckage in widening circles until he found Margaret. Her hands moved towards him a little as if she thought he might be able to help her to her feet. He crouched shuddering beside her, then covered her with the tattered remains of his leather coat.

'Walter.' The word was weak and slurred but he knew what she was trying to ask and he knew the answer he must give.

'Further down the hill,' he said. 'He'll be all right, but I didn't want to move him.'

A terrible sorrow flooded him as he knelt aching and shivering with shock. This was one half of the woman – the composite woman – he loved. What sort of Loving Hand had guided her to this? Gently he brushed the hair from her face. She was trying to speak again and he had to put his ear almost to her mouth to hear.

'I'm a terrible driver.'

'It wasn't you,' he said tearfully. 'They shot the car from under you. The tyres . . .'

'Tell Walter . . . I'm sorry . . .'

After a while her eyes closed.

He waited until he had no doubt that she was dead, then he began clambering numbly up the hill through the violated snow and the scorched trees.

Chapter Thirty-Nine

Comrade Zander walked to the nearest house and after asking the people there to report the accident he washed the blood from his face and borrowed a coat to cover his torn clothes.

It was almost noon when he reached the marriage bureau. After what seemed a very long time the door was opened by Fräulein Kopf. She was wearing her fur-trimmed coat and her gold-rimmed glasses. She looked as he had last seen her but something, he thought, will have gone out of her. When one thing changes, everything changes.

She saw the dressing on his face. 'What's happened, Freddi? Where are they?'

'They're dead,' he said.

'Dead?' She locked the door and stood with her back to it. 'What's happened?' she said again. She touched his face. 'Are you all right?'

All right? The question surprised him. He would never be all right again.

'You'd better let me renew that dressing. Your face is still bleeding.'

She took a first-aid box from her desk and turned on the gas water heater. As she bathed the cut he told her what had happened.

'It's awful,' she said. 'It's a miracle you got out of it so lightly.'

Lightly? That was something he would have to think about, something he couldn't assess as close to the event as this.

'I can't believe it,' she said. 'Both of them . . . but then, maybe . . .' She paused as if changing direction. 'I suppose they were in love.' It wasn't a question.

'Oh, yes,' he said with a twinge of pride that he couldn't have explained. 'They were in love.'

'Yet they couldn't have been happy, not really,' she said, as if in the marriage bureau she had, despite her denials, acquired a special insight into the dark places that abound round the edges of light. 'They had no real future. It seems an awful thing to say, but maybe this way they've suffered less.' She shivered as if at the dreadfulness of her judgment. 'I don't think we should wait any longer,' she said. 'There's nothing here any more.'

The desk top was bare and the calendar and the mirror had gone from the wall.

'No,' Comrade Zander said. 'Nothing.'

They went into the other room. The smell of the burning car was still with him. It was almost as if the smoke of it filled the grey corners. His head throbbed and the floorboards seemed soft and billowy under his feet. He felt that some essential part of him had been left in the snow beside Margaret.

Chapter Forty

Icy rain swept Berlin and around Woolcott's desk the light was chill.

Derby stared at the decoded message that Woolcott had handed him. He felt peculiarly cold and empty. His voice was hushed.

'They wanted you to call it off as well?'

Woolcott nodded almost furtively. His eyes had the red grittiness that comes from a night without sleep. 'It came too late. I'd have gone over there myself if there'd been time.' He sounded as if he was giving evidence in a court.

'Oh, no,' Derby groaned. 'He needn't have died at all, then? They could both still have been alive.'

'It came an hour after the girl went back to East Berlin,' Woolcott said. 'I spent the night trying to organise some way of contacting her . . . of calling Cavers off.'

Derby was staring over the top of the message at Woolcott as if he had never really seen him before. 'In the end, everybody was willing to let Eisler get away with it except you,' he said incredulously. He let the message flutter to the desk. 'Oh, Jesus,' he said with an intensity of regret that he could not understand. 'If only we'd been able to call Cavers off.'

'It's the girl I'm sorry about,' Woolcott said.

'And what about Eisler? Aren't you sorry about him?'

'Eisler?' Woolcott's expression suggested that he knew two or three people called Eisler. He sighed. 'Eisler was a silly idealist who threatened the peace of the world because he did not understand the nature of power or the care with which it must be exercised.'

Derby's shoulders rose and fell convulsively. 'God, is that all you can say about him?'

'No,' Woolcott said irritably. 'It isn't all I can say about him. I can add that Eisler got more out of life than he deserved. He became an international hero, then died young and tragically before he could be discredited. Most politicians would settle for that.'

'Oh, Jesus,' Derby groaned again. 'If only we'd been able to contact Cavers.'

Woolcott put his pipe down and sat looking at it, his hands clasped in front of him. 'It wouldn't have made any difference.'

Derby's mouth began to move but he did not speak. He waited with drawn eyebrows.

Woolcott hesitated, then seemed to decide to give the court a full confession. 'You see, there was more than just Cavers.'

Derby's glower deepened. 'If you'd been able to call Cavers off the girl would have brought Eisler out. He could have been in Lisbon by now.'

'She thought she was bringing him out.'

'Thought?' Derby sounded affronted.

Woolcott closed his eyes. 'Eisler was almost certainly dead before the car went off the road.'

Derby's face twisted in surprise. 'Cavers got him?'

'No.'

It took Derby perhaps ten seconds to work it out. At the end he looked as if he was going to be sick. 'Oh, my God,' he said. 'That poor girl.'

'Yes.' Woolcott's nod was sympathetic. 'I told you it was the girl I was sorry for.'

'You let her poison him for you,' Derby said in the way of a man enunciating an impossible proposition.

'She never knew.'

'No, but if your sniper had missed she would have

known.' Derby's voice was a snarl. 'Somewhere along the way she would have discovered Eisler was dead.' He got up and began walking about, muttering. 'You don't leave much to chance, do you, Woolcott?'

'I'm not paid to leave things to chance.'

'And you weren't paid to have Eisler bumped off, either.' A gleam of hope began to come through Derby's angry confusion. 'This isn't going to be very good for you, is it? What do you think they'll do to you? Will you last long enough now to qualify for your pension?'

Woolcott's expression was untroubled. It was as if, by confiding in Derby, he had attained his customary peace.

'I don't think they'll be too harsh,' he said. 'After all, it isn't the St Vincent de Paul Society we work for.' He leaned forward a little. 'All right, so I went out on a limb. But they knew, they *knew*, what was going on and the bastards were with me right up almost to the end. Anyway, Ramsden . . .' he began to look smug '. . . in our country we still have a sneaking regard for the maverick.'

Derby pushed both hands into his trouser pockets and went sombrely to the window. He stood looking out at the wet barracks wall and the dripping trees beyond.

'God,' he said with feeling. 'I'd hate to be an East German. It's going to be pretty dark again over there for another fifteen or twenty years.' He turned. 'Doesn't even that worry you? Or don't people matter?'

'Dry your eyes, Ramsden,' Woolcott said tolerantly. He crossed the room and joined Derby at the window. Rain glistened on the red tiles and bubble-glass windows of the quaint old houses along the street. Woolcott looked out appreciatively.

'Your sympathy is really quite indiscriminate, to-day,' he said quietly. 'Besides, you know people always matter with us. That's the big difference between us and the Communists.'